A LIFE ON THE LINE

Some warning intuition alerted Torp before he caught any actual sound of disturbance. Abruptly he swung his horse about, halting it and staring hard, his ears keened in intent listening.

He could see nothing in that direction except the dark black prairie, a star-fired sky above. For a moment he could hear nothing above the continuing noise of the herd. So strong was his feeling that trouble had developed, he began to ride rearward. In some five minutes he saw them, two riders coming cautiously from the cow camp.

There was only one thing to do then—try to turn them back and give Cal and his men every chance to get the cattle on to home range. When Torp had narrowed the gap between himself and the oncoming riders, he lifted his pistol out of the holster. He fired two shots, well above their heads, that served both as warning to them and to Cal. To his disappointment, the oncomers only lifted the speed of their horses to a lope and drove forward.

COMANCHE PRAIRIE

GIFF CHESHIRE

LEISURE BOOKS NEW YORK CITY

A LEISURE BOOK®

September 2005

Published by special arrangement with Golden West Literary Agency.

Dorchester Publishing Co., Inc.
200 Madison Avenue
New York, NY 10016

ISBN 0-8439-5573-2

The name "Leisure Books" and the stylized "L" with design are trademarks of Dorchester Publishing Co., Inc.

Printed in the United States of America.

Visit us on the web at www.dorchesterpub.com.

TABLE OF CONTENTS

No Man's Range

Giff Cheshire was born on a homestead in Cheshire, Oregon. The county was named for his grandfather who had crossed the plains in 1852 by wagon from Tennessee and the homestead was the same one his grandfather had claimed upon his arrival. Cheshire's early life was colored by the atmosphere of the old West that in the first decade of the new century had not yet been modified by the automobile. In 1929 he came to the Portland area in Oregon and from 1929 to 1943 he worked for the U.S. Corps of Engineers. By 1944, having moved to Beaverton, Oregon, he found he could make a living writing Western and North-Western short fiction for the magazine market and presently stories under the byline Giff Cheshire began appearing in *Lariat Story Magazine*, *Star Western*, and *North-West Romances*. His short story, "Strangers in the Evening" in *Zane Grey's Western Magazine* (10/49), won a Zane Grey Award that year. This story first appeared under the title "Never Let A Spitfire Go!" in *Star Western* (6/51). For its appearance here the author's original title has been restored.

I

"what i need i claim"

The oncoming riders looked hostile. Bart Tyler sat his saddle and watched them spill out of the gap and spur toward him. Of those four riders, Tyler figured that it was Matt Ginsing he'd have to kill. It had been shaping up that way for a year. Ginsing, Slash 3 ramrod, never rode off home range without a couple of hard-bitten hirelings.

Bart was on a slope, and a big cut of Herefords under his brand was shuffling down onto the bottom below him. It seemed like evening, although it was only a little past noon. The sooty atmosphere lent a glassy sheen to the frozen rock formations all about. The oncoming riders were not swinging over to come around the steers but were holding arrogantly to their course and driving head-on, hell-for-leather.

Bart thundered down in a wide hook to the left. His throat was dry and tight, for this was a thing he should never have run into up here at the edge of the *malpais*. Slash 3 lay well to the south, and Bart had no idea what Ginsing was doing here at the gap. It was no day for casual riding. A sudden freeze had come two days before. Now it had moderated with the wind in the north and that meant snow.

Bart came onto the flat without speeding up the slow shuffling of the numbed steers and pulled on ahead. Ginsing and his men seemed to sight them and swung off toward him. They slowed, then pulled to a stop, and let Bart come to them.

Ginsing was a tall, stooped man with red hair. The two

11

cowpunchers with him were the ones who usually accompanied him on his riding away from Slash 3. Bart thought he knew the fourth person, a small, slender girl who sat erectly in the saddle. She was dark and wore a tailored riding habit. She tallied with the description he had had of Linda Dana, the city girl who had fallen heir to Slash 3. Bart touched his hat out of deference to her, but his face was chilled by more than the frigid wind.

He looked at Ginsing and saw the ghost of a derisive grin on the man's mouth. "What are you doing in these parts, Ginsing?" Bart asked.

Matt Ginsing was pulling off a glove. He fished out the makings and began to shape a cigarette with one hand, in spite of the wind. A flashy handkerchief showed under the collar of his coat and he wore a fine-textured black hat. The girl was watching him shape the cigarette, and Bart wondered if Ginsing had the astuteness to realize her amusement was less at the performance than the show-off instinct behind it. Ginsing sealed the cigarette with a sweep of his tongue and took time to light up before he acknowledged that Bart had spoken. Then, instead of answering the question, he asked one. "You figure on holding them Herefords up here during the storm?"

"I'm not in the habit of walking them just for exercise."

"There won't be room for you in the brake shelters, Tyler," Ginsing said. "Slash Three is using them this year. We need the whole Crooked Creek bottom for the cut we brought in there yesterday. Wondered if you figured on it for yourself, so we come out to turn you back."

The icy wind seemed to stab clear through Bart. "Turn me back?" he said. "What are you driving at, Ginsing? What have you got Slash Three stuff in there for? You know damned well I've been using those brakes every year since I've been here!

12

The whole Crooked Creek bottom!"

"Watch your language!" Ginsing rasped.

Linda Dana smiled slightly. "I don't mind. I've an idea that, in his place, I'd use even stronger language than that."

Bart looked at her desperately. "I take it you're Linda Dana. Do you realize Slash Three's got no rights to the Crooked Creek bottom? Ginsing made a play for them last winter, but I talked him out of it. I thought that point was settled."

"Why," Linda said, "I understand that's a primitive area in there, that the government owns it."

"That's true, ma'am. But all these slope ranches have been using the back country for shelter during bad weather. We've sort of divvied up, each using the country behind it. Slash Three doesn't touch the *malpais*. In all the years your uncle ran it he never tried to horn in."

"But he had a right to," Linda said promptly. She waved a gloved hand toward the gap toward which Bart's steers still shuffled. "I understand, all right, that you've enjoyed the sole use of that part in there until now. But this winter it's our turn." She had taken the thing away from Ginsing and done it easily, and the ramrod was frowning a little.

Bart's temper let go completely at her easy dismissal of the matter. "By damn, you'll get your stuff out of those bottoms!" he thundered. "And you'll do it fast! I'm going in, and there's no room to spare. Ginsing knew that before he drove up here. You can dock his pay for the time and trouble."

Linda Dana smiled, and Bart saw a deep dimple sink in her cheek. "I was thinking that you should be turning yours back before they get mixed with our cattle in there. Do you want to turn them around and start for home, or do you want my men to do it for you?"

"You're asking for grief, ma'am. Slash Three never did set

13

too well with us little outfits. Your uncle was a hard-driven man, but he could be reasoned with. He was never as high-handed as Ginsing became once he took over. Ginsing's got this whole upper country on the prod. He's getting you into hot water."

Ginsing spurred his horse over. His two cowpunchers looked wary. Ginsing nodded to them and growled: "Go head back his steers."

"Lay-off!" Bart thundered. He saw that he had made no impression on Linda Dana with his appeal. She nodded her approval of Ginsing's order. The cowpunchers rode out. Bart was on the point of pulling his gun but held himself motionless. If he gave them the excuse, they would plug him, for Ginsing could shoot the way he rolled a one-handed cigarette and the cowpunchers were gunslingers.

Thoughtfully Linda Dana said: "My uncle wasn't a good businessman. Slash Three took on a lot of new stockers last fall. It hasn't shelter for them. And I don't see how you can argue it hasn't a right to take its turn at using the badlands. I know how you feel. I'm really sorry. But I couldn't help it if I would, could I?" She rode out after Ginsing's cowpunchers.

"In other words," Ginsing said, watching Bart guardedly, "the lady don't care a hoot if you and your critters freeze. She aims to have shelter for hers. I only work for her, Tyler."

"It sure must go against your grain," Bart rasped.

"I wouldn't say that." Ginsing struck out after the others.

The Slash 3 riders had turned Bart's Herefords away from the gap. Bart stood by his horse, numb with disbelief. There had been mean, over-bearing things from Matt Ginsing all through the year since Will Dana died, the mounting kind of clashes that could lead to killing trouble. The mounting impotence in Bart did nothing to cool his rancor. He sat motionless, letting them turn back his Herefords, only because the ghost of an idea was shaping in his mind. He could drive his herd back down to headquarters, letting it endure the full force of the oncoming storm and beyond doubt losing far more of it than he could afford. He could spend unending hours in the saddle trying to protect and care for it. He could forget Crooked Creek and its long and narrow bottoms, sheltered by the broken rises at the edge of the *malpais,* grassed, watered, and so well sheltered that a small herd could make out through weeks of blizzard untended. He could—but he wasn't going to, any more than any other man of pride would. "My uncle wasn't a good businessman," that fragile-looking, stone-hearted female had said, looking at him blandly with her amber-flecked eyes.

When they had turned Bart's steers, the Slash 3 riders headed back through the gap to Crooked Creek. So they meant to stick around and make sure he didn't try to move in there with them. There was the chance that he would enlist the other upper country ranchers to help him, which was why Ginsing had moved in there in force. Slash 3 would have to stay with its cattle through the undoubtedly coming blizzard, if that was any comfort.

Bart lacked the time to muster his neighbors, for the black sky showed plainly that snowfall was at hand. He stamped his feet on the hard ground, trying to warm them. Abruptly he swung and mounted his horse. The thing to do was to let them think he was buckling down and driving his bunch back home. But Tyler knew this reach of the badlands better than anyone else in the country. He knew of another way to reach Crooked Creek, farther up its length than Slash 3 was apt to penetrate. He swung in behind his slowly moving bunch and began to hurry it.

The steers picked up speed because they were moving downwind now. But even on Bart's back the wind had force enough to feel. He knew that Ginsing would be watching from the gap, but there was little chance of the man's guessing what he had in mind. For some reason Bart's anger had moved off Ginsing to center on Linda Dana. He was young, human, and fully conscious of her physical attractiveness.

The wind whipped up frequently in bitter gusts. The steers began to trot, to low in uneasiness, with the higher bawling of late calves outstanding and heart-touching. Weather like this always built a heavy dread in Bart Tyler, not only for its rigors and dangers, but because he had had a bad experience with it the winter before. He remembered now how close he had come to dying when he had lost his way in country he knew like the palm of his hand. A blinding snowstorm could do that, confusing a man, and turning him panicky, and destroying him. The first snowflake struck Bart's face. He frowned at the sky and saw the mounting agitation in the upper air. It was scattered with tiny, swirling dots that loomed larger as they fell. Then the flakes began to land on the neck and head of his horse and the ground about, and presently was obscuring the distant point of his little herd.

Bart had moved well away from the disputed gap. Presently, nearly lost in the obscurity, he made out the distant rim break he sought. He knew he would like this better once through it, with the vaulting roughs to break the blast of the wind and help guide him. There should be two or three hours of daylight left, and, as long as he could see a little, he could find his way where he wanted to go. He would figure out what to do with himself when he had settled the Herefords on upper Crooked Creek, for he had no camp outfit and might be unable to return home. But this last concerned him little in his hunger to defy Slash 3.

He rounded the herd and headed it through the escarpment break without trouble. Even in the first long cañon it was detectably warmer. Bart kept the bunch hustling, strung out and weary but as eager as he to move out of the blast. It kept getting darker and the snow was heavier. But Bart was easing, able now to guide himself and knowing landmarks well enough to feel confident of reaching his destination. The cañon narrowed constantly, the going getting rougher. Then suddenly it fanned out. They had come to the end of the big one. Bart halted his horse and sat for several minutes, hunched and with his gloved hands pressed in his armpits. Given a start here, the bunch would drift on into the long, narrow bottomland of upper Crooked Creek. Ordinarily he would leave them there to fend for themselves, looking in on them only when weather permitted. But with Slash 3 on down the creek and already turned hostile, he didn't dare leave them untended. Poor as the prospect looked, he had to go home and return with a camp outfit and spare horse or two.

He already was cold almost beyond feeling. He swung down and found his legs so stiff they nearly buckled. Holding onto the horse, Bart worked his knees and stamped his feet in the snow, which by now came halfway to his ankles. When he had warmed himself a little, he remounted and turned the horse about.

He had got as far as the escarpment break when the storm struck in full fury. Bart pulled in under an overhang and sat there for a long while, raw fear beginning to rise in him. It was strange how the scare like the one he had had could stick to a man. He was trembling and his shoulder muscles pulled into a hard lump. He knew that he could never make it home in this. He had to wait it out, with nothing much to help him. He wondered what Linda Dana thought of a blizzard now and what business principle she would use to meet it.

17

Knowing he could find fuel, water, and the best available shelter in the upper creek bottoms toward which he had started the herd, Bart turned back. He knew that full night had mixed into the blizzard's blackness long before he reached there. He found another overhang that was sheltered from the wind and big enough to protect him and the horse. He had difficulty in lifting his leg over to slide from the saddle, and, when he made it, he fell slackly into the deepening snow. Fear was eating openly at his nerves now, the panicked desire to mount again and ride headlong for home, and this was not mitigated by the unmistakable uneasiness of the animal.

He unsaddled the horse and hobbled it with clumsy, unfeeling hands. He took the saddle blanket, still warm from the horse's body, and wrapped it about himself. He was exhausted, growing languorous, but afraid to let go and rest. A man didn't dare because indifference came, then stupor, and abandonment to the mercy of the storm. He began to walk about.

He didn't know how many hours had passed when he grew aware that the wind's high howl was diminishing. When at last dawn began to lighten the snow-filled cañon about him, he realized that the snowfall had tapered off and showed signs of quitting completely. A sense of triumph came to Bart then, wiping out some of the bone-weary ache of his punished body. He was still alive, his horse was still on its feet, and this primitive victory gave him a kind of elation. Not till then did Bart come out of his lethargy enough to remember Matt Ginsing and Linda Dana and his defiance of them. He was cheered suddenly. He had kept his hands warm and he took the hobbles off the horse and threw on the saddle. For the first time in hours he rolled a cigarette to take the place of breakfast, then mounted, and rode into the cañon. The snow had completely wiped out the signs of his herd's passing and it was hours later when he broke out onto the creek bottom and saw his cattle there.

They were all right and would be if this was all there was to the storm. The creek was wooded, affording protected grazing and browse, and great patches of the exposed bottom grass had been swept clean. The only danger was from Slash 3. If Ginsing or one of his riders cared to poke far enough up the creek, discovery was certain. Ginsing wasn't a man to share this restricted hinterland graze after having laid claim to the shelter for Slash 3. If Ginsing got onto this, he would run the Herefords into the badlands or else out into the open sweeps.

Bart swung his gaze to the south. The creek pinched to a gorge there, narrow but negotiable, and some of his steers might stray that way, instinctively seeking the main bottom, with which they were familiar. Bart doubted that he dared leave them unherded even long enough to return to the ranch for a camp outfit and the extra horses he needed to spare the one he rode. A spunky, reckless thought came to him. The chances were good that Slash 3 had no idea of what he had done with his bunch. They must have made their own camp in the main bottom. They would have outriding to do there, after last night's fury. Bart had a sudden craving to outfit himself from their supplies or, if that wasn't possible, to destroy theirs and let them sweat it out as he had the night before.

Bart's familiarity with the region served him well as he rode down through the creek gorge and entered the big bottom. He meant at least to take a look at the Slash 3 camp. He swung to the right wall, picking his way carefully along the bottom, now passing large numbers of Slash 3 steers. He was growing tense, but his excitement was high and compelling.

Then he pulled his horse down in sudden interest. Far down the bottom three horsemen were riding away from him, heading toward the gap where the quarrel had taken place the day before. Bart couldn't tell who it was at that distance, but three cowpunchers would be plenty to tend the Slash 3 cattle and the lone disputer of its right to this shelter. Bart waited until distance had nearly dissolved the men, then turned his horse out into the bottom.

He came to the creek and moved through the trees, figuring they would have taken the campsite he had used on occasion. Presently he spotted the smoke of a fire ahead of him. He stayed on his horse and soon could see the camp. There was a tent, he saw, heavily weighted with the snow that had fallen in the night. On beyond was a rope corral holding several spare horses. But otherwise the site looked deserted. Bart rode in and swung down at the fire.

There was a coffee pot on a rock beside the still brisk fire, a savory-smelling kettle on a rod above it. Hunger hit Bart then. He found a cup and poured himself coffee. He was drinking it when he saw the tent flaps stir slightly. There was no wind in this sheltered place, and his gun hand brushed the grips of his .45 in a reflex action. He pulled the hand up in embarrassment when the flaps parted and Linda Dana stepped out.

Bart grinned at her, knowing that all the dislike he felt for her showed through the mock amusement. "You nearly made me swallow this coffee cup," he told her. "A man would think you'd have sense enough to hustle back to that nice big house at Slash Three yesterday. Apparently you've got a taste for roughing it."

"Apparently," said Linda, "you have a taste for other people's food."

"In this country grub belongs to anybody who needs it. I

20

need it. Naturally I expect to pay for it now that I've seen you here." That brought a flush to her cheeks that gave Bart pleasure. "How come you stayed out here?"

"The storm struck sooner than we figured. Ginsing said we didn't dare risk trying to get home till it had blown over."

"Don't blame him," Bart said.

She straightened and her head went back. She had pulled on a wool coat and had a muffler wrapped about her neck, a stocking cap on her head. She had caught his innuendo and was furious but too proud to answer. "I intend to learn the cattle business," Linda said. "That's why I came out with the men. I won't have hired help doing anything I'm too soft to do for myself. However, it was not my intention to play house with three men. And if I were a man, I would rip out your tongue for that remark."

"Where's Ginsing heading?" Bart drawled.

"They'll be back shortly. But if you have any further business with Slash Three, you can take it up with me."

"Fine and dandy, ma'am." Recklessness was stirring in Bart again. He had to act fast and get away before Ginsing and his cowpunchers returned. But his tracks would tell them plainly where he had come from to reach this camp and an hour's ride would show them the Herefords in the upper bottom. "You and me have got business. I aim to make a camp pack, for which in due time I'll pay you fully. And I don't aim to let Matt Ginsing know who did it."

"He'll know, all right," Linda retorted.

"Who'll tell him? Those horses yonder?"

She stared for an instant. "What do you mean?"

"You and me're going for a ride, ma'am."

"You're . . . abducting me?"

"Don't know about that. But I've got a mighty important reason to keep Ginsing from knowing who raided his camp.

21

Owlhooters ride through here. I figured to make it look like one of them had located the camp and helped himself. I've still got to make it look like that."

"Why . . . ?" Linda's face was white with disbelief.

"Don't worry, ma'am. I'd take you down to Slash Three if I figured there was no danger of you seeing Ginsing till this storm's blown over for sure."

"And since you can't . . . what?"

"I reckon we'll figure it out as we go along."

Linda's hand was moving slowly toward the pocket of her coat. It was a greenhorn movement; a Western girl would have known that he would notice. He stepped forward and caught her wrist. He fished the little gun from her pocket and slid it into his own. He remembered the wild desire that had burned in him the day before, to catch her in a plight as helpless as the one he had been in. Suddenly he felt no pity for her in her obvious fear.

She breathed: "So it's true! Everything I've heard about you!"

He looked at her in surprise. "How come you'd hear anything at all about a measly greasy-sacker like me?"

"I've heard plenty," Linda answered. "About you and all the other little ranchers who've fattened off Slash Three all these years!"

Bart's eyes had narrowed. "And you heard every word of it from Matt Ginsing. Woman, you're a plain damn' fool. Now, you move out there in the snow where I can look at your pretty figure. If you get wild impulses, I'll do more than wash your face in the snow. I'm going to make up a pack. I'm going to leave a note thanking Ginsing for the grub and blankets and the nice, pretty girl. Then we're going to do some wild riding, meandering so as to keep them busy a while trying to follow. I know this country and they don't. If I can fool them

22

the way I want, I'll figure out a better life for you."

"You . . . !" Linda said savagely. "You're the damned fool if you think you can get away with a thing like this!"

Never taking his eyes off her for long, Bart set about his business. There was a very real need in what he was doing, in addition to his personal feeling in it. He had to fool Ginsing about who had visited the camp, which would be impossible if he left Linda there. But it might be good for her, he reflected. She needed to learn how one of those fat little greasy-sackers had to live sometimes in the interest of his little herd. He took Slash 3's tarp and began to build an outfit, helping himself lavishly. He took their coffee pot, a skillet, and a hand axe. He went into the tent for a second and got the blankets off the cot Linda had used. When he went to the rope corral and snaked out a pack pony and saddle horse, he forced her to accompany him, stumbling through the snow. She was silent, submissive, and genuinely frightened. If there had been any doubt about what she had been told of him, there was none now. Presently he made her step up into the saddle, gave her a blanket to wrap about herself, and they rode out. He had decided against leaving the note he had threatened to leave, figuring he could make the horses' tracks tell the story more convincingly. The single tracks he had made coming down from the upper bottom would be less interesting to Ginsing than double tracks going on in another direction. With Linda missing, Ginsing would be quick enough to assume that it had been an owlhooter coming in from the heart of the *malpais,* finding a chance to re-outfit and acquire a pretty girl as well. Slash 3 would ride the other tracks in the effort to liberate Linda, and Bart intended to make it hard riding. He headed due west, into the roughest kind of country.

II

"cold solitude"

A grim satisfaction came to Bart as he considered what he had imposed upon Matt Ginsing to balance the hopelessly unequal situation. There would be the shock and alarm of Linda's disappearance, a sudden dangerous shortage of provisions, and the urgent need of pursuit into wild and forbidding country of which Ginsing and his riders had only the scantest knowledge. Bart knew he could play hare and hounds with Slash 3 for days on end, keeping them always away from his own herd.

They climbed through a rim break, making no effort to hide their trail. Bart wanted to be followed, to force his enemies to exhaust themselves, and taste of the hopelessness they had forced on him. He had no pity for Linda Dana, abject and frightened though she was, because of them all she most needed a dose of that bitter medicine. When he had planted enough trail to keep them busy for a few days, Bart aimed to take her out. If that brought his cattle safely through this stretch of bad weather, he meant thereafter to mobilize his neighbors and force a showdown with Slash 3. If she wanted to sick the law on him for abduction, that was all right with Bart Tyler.

They kept going all through that day and Bart knew he was giving Linda a ride she had never dreamed could be. He pressed even deeper into the roughs, floundering through snowdrifts, wandering with the aimlessness of the lost. Twice he bisected their own trail, once heading south and again going north, to compound the confusion for Matt Ginsing. The day stayed clear, and, as the afternoon waned, Bart made a wide loop and began to back trail. In the thickening twilight he found shelter for a camp and halted. His first stab of sympathy for Linda hit him when he had to help her from the saddle and hold her upright, tramping through the snow until she had worked the numbness out of her body. But he kept his resolve firm. Only the day before she had told him through Ginsing that he and his steers could freeze to death without causing her concern. She was getting a taste of what that meant. Perhaps she realized that she had asked for it and it was that which kept her so tractable and quiet.

Bart unpacked, hobbled the horses, and made camp. They were under another overhang, with a sheer rock wall to the windward. He took the hand axe and found fuel, then set a fire out from the wall to give them the warm space between. It was free of snow, and Linda dropped down in complete exhaustion.

He tossed her the blankets and said: "Wrap yourself up. You'll be warm as a new biscuit pretty soon. I'd give you back your gun except it wouldn't do you any good. If you killed me, you'd only rattle around in these roughs till you died yourself."

Linda seemed to wince, then she threw back her pert head in total hostility. "You should be getting a lot of satisfaction out of this, Bart Tyler!" she blazed.

"I reckon I should," he agreed, "but I don't aim to. Don't forget, ma'am, that you had me completely helpless back there at the gap. You showed no mercy."

"And I don't expect any now!" she retorted.

"You'll get it in the way you keep worrying about," he said, and he grinned at her. "We've laid enough trail to keep that red-headed foreman of yours busy for three or four days.

In the morning we're pulling out and I'll take you home."

"Then what? Do you realize I'll have you in jail?"

"Maybe, but not if I can help it. Slash Three has declared war on the little ranches that lay around it. I aim to have a powwow with them and see what they aim to do about that."

Linda's lips parted in a scornful smile. "So the parasites will now unite to destroy the ranch they've fed on all these years."

Bart had dropped the pack from the pack pony and was making camp. He looked at her sharply. "That's twice you've graveled about us two-bitters. Ginsing sure must have fed you a lot of lies. Just what is it you've got against us, Miss Linda?"

Her answer was prompt, attesting that she had thought a lot about it. "My uncle should have been a rich man with the holdings he had and the hard work he did all his life. And he died from financial worry and close to bankruptcy, bled white by rustling from you parasites. Harassed and hampered at every turn because you little outfits hate the big ones."

"Slash Three is near bankruptcy?" Bart asked in disbelief.

"Why would I try to lie about it, if it wasn't?"

Bart was starting to cook their supper, slicing the bacon he had taken from a can, and dropping the slices into a heating frying pan. He filled the coffee pot with snow and set it next to the fire to melt down to water. What Linda had said interested him powerfully and he gave it considerable thought.

"It's sure news to me that your uncle was having money trouble," he said finally. "I reckon somebody's made you believe it, but that talk about rustling and trouble-making from us little outfits is pure hot air."

Her smile was bitter. "What else would you say to me?"

Bart ground coffee beans on a rock, using the butt of his pistol, and started coffee. He had taken a jar of sourdough from the Slash 3 camp, and he poured some into the skillet, and set it to bake in the heat of the fire. He was puzzled, disturbed by what she had said, and she seemed to prefer silence. When he had supper cooked, he filled a tin plate and handed it to her.

"You'll feel better with some hot grub in you."

Temper seemed to prompt her to refuse the food, then she accepted it. Bart nearly grinned at the hungry way she ate. It seemed to revive her and lift her spirits, the way good food could when a person was beaten-out and miserable. But it brought no trace of relenting into her manner. Watching her covertly, Bart was struck with the thought that he might have misjudged her, that she believed what she had been told and had considered her action back there at the gap justified. But that made no difference to his own plans. He had his steers to protect, and he had to keep her away from Ginsing until he could take stronger steps against the man.

It did make a difference in his attitude toward her. In the kindest tone he had used to her, he said: "Since I don't mean to let you see Ginsing for a while, I can tell you why I'm doing this. I ran my herd into the Crooked Creek bottom on up the creek from where you people were. I rode for wages till I was twenty-five, and I've put in five more years trying to get a start on my own. If I lose my herd, it's all wiped out. And I sure stood to lose it the other day, and by your decision. I still stand to lose it if Ginsing finds it in there. So I did what I did to keep him tied up and thinking about something else."

Linda was looking at him and listening and there was the merest chance that she was impressed. But she said nothing whatsoever. Night was about them now, and a cold moon had emerged in a clear sky. Bart took the saddle blankets and let Linda have the better bedding from her own camp. He said: "Now relax and get some sleep. I hope you've got more sense

27

than to try and get away. You wouldn't get far, and, if it happened to snow again, neither I nor anybody else could trail you. I need sleep myself and I don't want to worry about you."

"I'm no fool," Linda answered.

"Maybe not," Bart agreed, and found that he really meant it.

He bedded down at a respectable distance from the bed he made for the girl. She kept by the fire for a long while but rolled up in her blankets finally and he relaxed. He was certain Ginsing had told her a lot of wild yarns about the neighboring ranches and their relations with Slash 3. He was equally sure that she had somehow gained the wrong impression about the big outfit's financial standing. A cowman with only one eye could see that Slash 3 made money and always had, that it was managed too closely and well to get itself into trouble, and it had suffered no severe adversities in the years Bart had lived on its border.

He didn't know how her uncle's estate had been handled, by whom administered, or what kind of financial accounting had been made to her when she inherited the ranch. But Bart would have bet his imperiled little herd that she had been fooled, and badly, and for a reason. Somewhere in recent hours his conception of Linda had changed. She was green as a pond frog and suddenly possessed of a vast property. She obviously didn't know just how vast and rich it was. There was only one conclusion and Bart drew it now. Somebody meant to take over what had been kept hidden from her. Matt Ginsing had at least a big part in it. The discovery gave Bart a strange sense of bewilderment. He had bought chips in that game without realizing it and would have to play out the hand.

Bart roused frequently to refreshen the fire and make sure

that impulse did not cause Linda to attempt an escape. But each time he rose she lay dead to the world. He was glad of that, for as the night advanced the wind began again and hourly increased its howling intensity. Bart's worry increased with it, his old fear of a blizzard revived in him. He had gambled on fair weather until he had Linda out of here. A sudden change for the worse would catch them in a plight he couldn't bear to contemplate.

Long before dawn he saw the first snowflake drift down through the outer light of the campfire. Alarm ran through him, wild and close to panic. He had made his bet and lost it and they were in for trouble. His glance fell on the sleeping Linda and remorse rose in him. He had gambled a life that didn't belong to him. He had learned too late that he well could have been blinded by outrage and suspicion. But he shook these weakening thoughts out of his mind. He had to meet the situation and second-guessing was of no use.

It meant that they had to strike out at once, heading for the outside. He roused Linda, saying: "It's started snowing. We've got to hit the saddle. With no breakfast."

She made a low, moaning sound and for a moment more lay still. Then she scrambled up, the fear in her jumping to him and intensifying his own. He willed himself to a steady coolness and was glad that somebody outside himself had need of him. He said: "Try to make up the pack while I saddle up. The sky's still pretty clear. It's just that we'd better not risk getting pegged down here."

The need to keep her reassured was good for him, too. Linda made a couple of wild turns around the fire, got hold of herself, and began to gather the pack. Bart unhobbled the horses and saddled them.

They had traveled for an hour when daylight began to

29

lighten the atmosphere. The snowfall was heavier but still little more than a drizzle, a light but steady sifting. Bart was heading directly for the rim gap by which he had sneaked his herd into upper Crooked Creek bottom. If they made it, he would be in territory more familiar to him and would stand a better chance, even if this thing whipped up to blizzard fury again. He broke trail for Linda, leading the pack horse, and had dropped all worry about her keeping close to him. Her fear of the surrounding wilderness and glowering sky was all too evident. She crowded her horse as close to Bart as she could manage.

To Bart she had become a different personality to the one he had detected at the start. She had firmly believed Slash 3 to be a struggling, hard-pressed spread in the midst of enemies. It didn't seem so callous to Bart now that she had insisted on her ranch taking its turn in the Crooked Creek shelter, and he couldn't censure her for being so badly fooled in a business about which she knew nothing. He had to admit that he was sorry for her and for what he had done to her out of rancor. It was the least he could admit. Bart had his own fears to fight down and he forced himself to pick a careful, strength-saving route. He made no mention of it to Linda, but with each passing hour the visible distance grew less, the snowfall heavier, the sky darker. There was no sign of the sun, but he figured it was late afternoon when they dropped down into the cañon through which he had brought his cattle coming in.

He halted. Linda floundered up beside him. Both saddlers and the pack horse were nearly exhausted from the daylong struggle with the underfooting. Night was just ahead of them. It was a long way to his ranch and a longer way to Slash 3. Only the winter before he had got lost while out in the open and had nearly died.

Before he could speak, Linda said: "We won't make it, will we?"

"Not as far as I hoped," Bart admitted.

"You don't know how I loathe you for forcing me into this." It seemed to be said without passion, and this very coldness struck deeply into Bart.

III

"bitter amends"

He turned his horse without answering, knowing that their best chance lay in striking deeper into the *malpais* and coming again to where he had left his steers in upper Crooked Creek bottom. It was as sheltered as any place in here and in addition afforded firewood and water and even fresh beef if they were storm-bound long enough to need it. Linda followed him numbly and Bart could no longer bear to think of her and what, out of pure resentment, he had done to her.

It was not long after that when Bart grew aware that night and all its greater terrors were coming in upon them again. But by then the snow was a heavy, pelting force, cutting visibility to a point not over a hundred yards ahead of them. He rode on doggedly, only now and then flinging back to see that Linda followed. They came to a cañon that lay with the wind and had the full cold blast to buck. Because she was downwind from him, he didn't hear anything when it happened. He just looked back and saw the empty saddle of her horse.

Bart halted his own jaded mount and flung himself from the saddle. It didn't surprise him when he went on down, landing full length in the heavy snow carpet. He staggered to his feet and wallowed back past the pack pony and Linda's still plodding horse. He couldn't see her because of the snowfall and the night. He followed the dragging trail the animals had made and then found her, still and silent, where she had hit the snow when she had fallen from the saddle.

He bent, self-reproof releasing some spring of energy in

him. But she was light when he swung her up into his arms and staggered back along his own path. Her horse had halted behind the pack pony and Bart's own. He had come up to it before he realized that she could not ride and that neither horse was strong enough to carry double in this underfooting. He thought of lashing her across the saddle in dead weight, a punishing and dangerous thing to her in this condition. He tried to think where they were, but landmarks were blotted out. It probably was still a considerable distance to the Crooked Creek bottomland. He placed Linda in the snow, then strung her horse and pack pony behind his horse, tied together. He got Linda across his shoulders, his left arm snuggling her knees to him, the hand catching her limp arm. He caught the reins in his free hand and started on, heading fully into the wind. Presently he was moving through total darkness. There was no fuel in here but Bart knew then that he had to find the best shelter he could.

He veered to the right, coming to the talus of the wall rise. He followed this, rocky and rough though it was. But the increasing size of the detritus began to tell him where they were and his heart sank. It was a long way yet to the creek bottom. But it helped decide him. Presently he grew aware that the strong headwind had been cut off. He knew that the cañon narrowed some place in here between high, nearly vertical walls. Protection from that freezing wind was the best he could hope for. He halted when they came to a rock nest that would be additional protection, and again he put Linda down.

His sense of lightness at the released weight gave him a surprise. He used his numbed feet to clear the snow back from the base of a big boulder. He seemed warmer already from having gotten out of the beat of the wind. He unsaddled the horses but left their blankets on them, his mind dull but remembering to hobble them in case they would be needed again. He used the other blankets to make a bed as far in under the big boulder as he could get it. He laid Linda there.

She was too cold and in this condition her temperature would keep dropping the few degrees it took to be fatal to human life. He had matches and could burn the pack saddle for a fire that would last only a uselessly short while. But he was warm, almost comfortable now from his exertions. He unbuttoned her coat and then his own and slipped into the blankets beside her. He pulled her close to him to give her his body's warmth. The wind howled and shrieked above but could not touch them. The blankets trapped their warmth and presently he knew that her breathing was less shallow.

He came out of a torpor a long time later to realize she was struggling in the tight clutch of his arms. Before he had fully remembered the situation, he felt her teeth sink into his chin. He released her hastily, gasping: "Cut it out, you little fool! You came within an inch of freezing to death."

She struggled away from him, and he climbed to his knees, suddenly furious. If she thought he had taken advantage of her helplessness, he should have let her keep on thinking so. If she preferred to freeze, she could damned well freeze. But the air into which he rose was bitterly cold, its chill going through him in a knifing sweep. The horses needed the flimsy protection of their saddle blankets. Reconsidering, Bart dropped to sit beside her.

He said: "Look, Linda, you blacked out and fell off your horse. I carried you as far as I could but couldn't make it to where I wanted. I had to get you warm and there's no wood around."

"You carried me?" Linda asked.

"It was that or lash you head down across a saddle. But if

you're still of a mind to let me freeze, just consider how you're going to get out of here on your lonesome."

She said nothing, and he covered himself again beside her. Presently her relaxing body settled against him, and he knew she was asleep. He thought: *If we live, I'm going to have an awful time getting her out of my mind. But I'll have to. She hates me worse than poison.* . . .

The storm was still wild and raging when daylight washed out some of its obscurity. Bart climbed to his feet, knowing they had to press on for the creek bottom where they could have a fire and hot food and feed for the horses. He rose and swore involuntarily.

"What's the matter?" Linda gasped from under the blankets. She rolled out from under the boulder and rose hastily.

Bart pointed to the still and stiffened shape of a horse at a distance from them. "He did what we could have done. Just laid down and gave up and froze to death. The others kept stirring. We'll get on. There's enough light we can get to a better camp."

Linda was staring at the dead horse. Finally she said: "I'm sorry I made a fool of myself. I'm grateful for what you did for me."

He managed to grin at her. "Miss, you're learning a little about the cattle business."

Bart repacked the pack pony because it had been less heavily burdened than the saddle horses and was in better shape. But he led his own horse, and they started on afoot. It was brutal punishment when they came again into the full blast of the icy wind, but there was no escaping it. Once more they reached the place where the cañon fanned out and Bart knew they were close to the bottomland. He turned along the foot of the high bluffs, once more out of the wind. Hope was rising in him. If they could find suitable shelter, they had every chance of coming through.

They kept going. At long last Bart found what he sought, a wind-eroded half cave in the sandstone bluff. The walking, since they had got out of the wind, had warmed them, and even Linda let out a little cry of relief.

Bart made camp hastily for they had not eaten that day or the day before. He took the hand axe and went out and presently was back with enough wood to get a fire started. He built the fire and watched her unpack, almost child-like in her eagerness. She had bacon sliced by the time he had a hot frying pan. Without being told, she melted down snow for coffee, and, when he started to make their bread, she said: "Let me." So he took the axe and went out and brought in a bigger supply of wood.

He had a smoke with his coffee after they had eaten. Something was working on him, and he said: "I gave you a rough time, didn't I?"

She looked at him, and now he was quite sure that the bitter hostility had left her eyes. She said: "Maybe."

"That's a queer answer. What do you mean?"

"I gave you a rough one, too, didn't I? Actually, I started all this. And a rough time isn't so bad if you've got the sense to learn something from it."

"What have you learned?" Bart asked with interest.

"That nothing on earth tastes as good as bacon, skillet bread and butter, and sandy black coffee. That it's darned nice to be alive. And that people ought not to get their judgments second-hand."

Bart smiled. "People who make their own can still land a mile wide of the mark."

"If that's an acknowledgment of guilt, I'm glad. I was

going to be too noble to say so, but I still don't think I'm the only damned fool in this situation."

They were storm-bound through that day and night, but Bart rose on the following morning to find that the snowfall had stopped. The sky was clear. A long slope ran from the cliffs to the distant creek. Away from the cliffs the wind had kept great patches of grass swept clean. He saw the horses grazing in the near distance, and all along the open reach his strung-out Herefords. A deep satisfaction came to him. His herd was all right, although his concern for it had faded in the anxieties of the last few days. Now Bart must think again of Matt Ginsing and his hard-faced riders.

He returned to the campfire to find that Linda had awakened. He hadn't told her how close they were to the Slash 3 camp, and he wondered if he should and let her make her own decision about returning there and exposing him to Ginsing. She had changed greatly, but he didn't know how much or for how long. Things might look differently to her now that they seemed to be safe.

He decided to feel her out a little before going too far. "Did Ginsing ever say anything to indicate he might like to buy Slash Three," he asked, "or otherwise take the poor, money-losing proposition off your hands?"

She glanced at him sharply. "Why do you ask?"

"He must have had some reason for lying his head off to you. That outfit's a going concern and always has been. What trouble it ever had with its neighbors, it started. In a country like this, people get to know a lot about each other's business affairs. Somebody wants to get you plenty sick of your inheritance, Miss Linda, and wants to get the whole of it at a nice cheap price. Who but the man who fed you the lies? Matt Ginsing?"

"All right," she said, "Ginsing wants to buy Slash Three. He thinks that, if it was run right, it could pull out of the mess. I know how much cash I came by. It's hardly enough to meet the payroll and other expenses though the winter."

"Because your uncle was a great one to put his money back into the spread," Bart snapped. "That's the way he built it. But what you don't know is how much the place is worth or how much cattle you could tally if you got honest figures. Somebody gave you a false appraisal."

"You really mean that?" Linda asked. From her surprise Bart knew she hadn't even suspected such a thing like that

"Who administered your uncle's estate?"

It was a moment before she answered. Then she swallowed and said: "Matt Ginsing. You probably know my uncle was sick a couple of years before he died. He turned everything over to Ginsing and fixed it so the man would run things until I'd learned enough about it to take over."

"And there," Bart said, "is your answer. You don't have to take my word for it. Get the court to order an honest accounting and you'll be surprised at how rich you are and how little need there is for you to fight your way out of the mess your dinky little neighbors got you into. Ginsing wants to start trouble with us to make it all the more discouraging for a greenhorn girl. That's why he rooted me out of my shelter this winter."

Linda's cheeks had blanched and her voice sounded a little shaken. "I just can't believe that," she gasped.

"Find out for yourself," Bart told her. "Slash Three camp isn't very far from here. I can take you there and let you spoil my little caper here. Or I can take you on home."

"Take me home," she said, without hesitation.

Bart wanted to take a look at the cattle before tackling that. He took a rope and walked out and caught his horse. It appeared to be in good shape. He brought it in and saddled it, then rode out through snow that was at times knee-deep, at times swept clean, and sometimes piled so high it bogged his horse. He worked his way through the scattered Herefords, finding a few downed cows that he tailed up and a couple of late calves that had died in the storm. That didn't depress him because every storm took its toll and he expected it.

He was down toward the gorge that formed the connection between here and the lower bottom when he pulled down his horse in sudden interest. He wasn't sure what he had seen, but, as he studied the dazzling white distance, he recognized the small shapes of horsemen. Three of them and coming toward him. Bart's brow knit in a dark frown. It had to be Slash 3, and they probably had sighted the Herefords already.

IV

"i've turned greasy-sacker"

He knew what had happened. When Ginsing had returned to his camp to find Linda missing, he had seen single horse tracks coming there from this direction. When the resumed blizzard had cut off the possibility of continuing the search for her, Slash 3 had returned to camp. Now all tracks were wiped out, deeply buried in fresh snow. So Ginsing had remembered and got to wondering what lay in this direction. Bart knew this was the showdown. There was no hiding the Herefords, or even Linda. Ginsing's wrath would be doubled when he knew for sure who had abducted her. Bart looked at his gun and found it in working order. Waiting, he slipped his hands into his armpits to warm them. The oncomers grew more discernible in the distance.

He saw from their manner presently that they had spotted him. He was sure now that it was Ginsing and both his cowpunchers. Bart knew that gun trouble was bound to come and had the impulse to cut loose at this distance to drive them back out of this bottom and warn them against giving him more trouble. But legally, if not in fact, it was Linda's right to say what was to be done with the Herefords and with Bart Tyler himself. Bart waited.

The others rode up to him, slowly and awkwardly, in the snow. Matt Ginsing's eyes were fairly withering in their hostility.

He growled: "So it was you, Tyler! Damn your mangy hide, you've got a gut-drilling coming!"

"Take it easy, Ginsing," Bart said softly. "I've got nothing coming from you. But if you feel otherwise, you'll get as good as you send."

"Where's Linda Dana?"

"Keeping house for me, Ginsing. And she's got her eyes open to you finally. Your rotten scheme won't work. You'd better let your hackles down and stay away from her unless you're in a hurry to get fired."

"Where's your camp?" Ginsing thundered.

"It could be anywhere," Bart said, grinning. "I came a long piece to take a look at my Herefords. In case you think the three of you can put a slug in me, stop and ask yourselves how you'd ever find her if you did. It's a big *malpais* and a mean one."

"By damn, we'll pry it out of you!" Ginsing blustered. "I see what you're up to. You've thrown sand in that girl's eyes. You figure you can marry her and come by Slash Three. Even if she's willing, you're not going to cut it." Something cold and merciless showed in the man's eyes. Playing for high stakes, as Bart had no doubt he was, the last days must have been an ordeal for him.

Ginsing gave his cowpunchers the merest signal. By habit they kept their horses spread out. Bart saw three hands streaking for gun grips, and he jumped his horse straight at Ginsing, who was closest. He pulled his own gun but doubted that he had time. The two horses crashed together, and Ginsing's went down in the loose footing. Bart hurled himself toward the man, which was the only thing that could keep the cowpunchers from shooting at him pointblank. They rolled free of the tangled horses together, each man trying to use his gun.

Ginsing's exploded and Bart felt its muzzle's heat on his cheek. He used his elbow to hit the man across the chin, then balanced, whipped the barrel of his gun across Ginsing's head. He rolled on into the snow, still clinging to Ginsing. The horses got untangled and scampered away. The two cowpunchers were circling, hunting an angle from which they could shoot at Bart without endangering their leader. One of them tried a shot that went high. Bart shoved his gun into Ginsing's ribs and yelled: "Drop those sixes or I plug him!"

"Plug the son-of-a-bitch!" the ugly-faced one bawled.

"Shut up, Jack!" the other cut in. "Tyler'd do it. Ginsing lost his head. Tyler, we made a mistake. Me and Jack'll holster our guns and we'll all start over." True to his word, he did it. Although the other cowpuncher still glowered, he followed suit.

Bart rose to a hunker but kept his gun in hand. He rapped: "You two jack dandies light your shucks. I'm keeping Matt Ginsing. He's going to set in on a powwow at my camp pretty soon. Don't try to follow me and don't try to attack my camp or the promises Ginsing must have made you won't be worth two cents."

The Slash 3 cowpunchers stared at each other. The more level-headed one nodded and they rode away, heading back toward the gorge. Ginsing was out cold. His horse and Bart's had not gone far in the heavy snow. Bart walked out and got them. He was less considerate than he had been with Linda. He threw Ginsing roughly across the saddle, tied him there, and started in to camp.

Not until he was on the last slope did Bart realize that Linda could have seen it all and must have heard those gunshots. It didn't surprise him to find her anxious-eyed and waiting when he rode up to the sandstone cave, leading Ginsing's horse and its burden.

"I saw it," she breathed. "Did you kill him?"

"No, worse luck. But you and me and Ginsing are going to come to an agreement about this bottomland."

"Ginsing has nothing to say about it. Slash Three is mine."

Bart watched her with a building smile. "Then who's going to use the Crooked Creek bottoms?"

"We are."

The smile left Bart's face. "I thought . . . !"

"Sorry," Linda cut in. "That's the best I can do. Can we go home now?"

Bart nodded and began to break camp. By the time he had the pack made up, Ginsing was beginning to revive. Bart had taken the man's gun and unloaded it and thrown the gun off into the snow. When, groaning, Ginsing shoved to a groggy sitting position, Linda crossed to him.

She said: "Hello. Did you have a nice nap?"

Ginsing's face was heavy with animosity. "So you think it's funny!" he snarled. "Me and the boys go through hell and high water for you, and you think it's a laugh!"

"No," Linda said, "I'm not amused. It's not entertaining to watch three men I've trusted trying to shoot down one greasy-sacker who only wants to protect his cattle. You didn't know I was watching, did you?"

"Tyler started it!" Ginsing growled. "He got tough. We had to pull his fangs to keep him from hurting somebody."

"Tyler didn't get tough," Linda retorted. "He was tough already. Tough enough to take the worst you could dish out and still make a monkey out of you. Ginsing, I'm asking the court to order an investigation of my uncle's estate and the way it was handled while you were administrator. I don't think you and I would be congenial with that going on. Do you want to quit or shall I fire you?"

Shock showed on Ginsing's face. "Who's going to run

the outfit for you? Tyler, there?"

"I'll worry about that."

"Everyone of the boys'll quit with me," Ginsing threatened.

"Fine. I'll be a one-woman outfit. A greasy-sacker."

Ginsing got drunkenly to his feet. His horse still stood near, and, when Bart made no objection, Ginsing strode to it and swung up. He didn't look at them as he rode out.

Bart looked worried. "Maybe you shouldn't have threatened him with that investigation, Miss Linda. It threw the worst scare into him he's had yet."

"What's wrong with scaring him?"

"He knows he's not going to fool you into selling out to him," Bart answered. "But it's hard telling what he's done and what all he wants kept covered up."

"He's not going to keep anything covered up," Linda retorted. "How could he?"

"He might keep you from ever going to anybody with anything."

Linda's eyes widened, then she swallowed. "He'd have to kill me."

"Yeah," Bart said.

He gave Linda his horse and took the bareback pack pony for himself, saying: "If you hear a shot, dive into the snow. They'd try to get me first."

"Oh, Bart," Linda breathed, and it was the first time she had ever used his first name.

They got through the roughs without trouble. Bart hadn't expected it there for Ginsing wasn't familiar with them. But he could guess the point at which Ginsing and his two cowpunchers could be expected to emerge. It was there that Bart feared trouble. But he said nothing of this to Linda. When they reached a rim break opening onto the outer plateau, he told her to drop behind him a distance, and rode on.

44

He swept out between the jaws of the high rim with his gun in his hand. The wisdom of that was attested when he heard the sharp crack of a carbine. His hat sailed from his head. The man was on his left, still mounted, his horse held close to the rim rock. Ginsing himself. He had a murder to accomplish and apparently didn't want his underlings to have knowledge of it. The carbine was still at Ginsing's shoulder. It fired again, a crowding determined shot, just as Bart chopped down with his gun and pulled the trigger. Ginsing pitched from the saddle. Bart rode over and stood above the dead man for a long moment. His having guessed the situation and swung into it alone and prepared for action had rattled Ginsing or Bart Tyler would by now be dead. He saw that Linda was coming on, regardless, and he didn't want her to see Ginsing. Bart swung up and rode out to meet her. She didn't have to be told what had happened. Bart said: "He tried a risky thing and decided to do it on his lonesome. His picked gunmen will clear out because they backed him too strongly in too many things. I'll take you to town. You'll have to locate a new foreman and have him pick up a new crew." He caught Ginsing's horse because he wanted a saddle under him, and he stopped to pick up his hat. They rode on.

The sky stayed clear now, and the wind was down. When they were well away from the scene of the violence, Linda said: "Bart, about that bottomland. When I said *we* would use it, you must have thought I meant Slash Three."

"Who did you mean?" he demanded.

"You and me. You've got to help me run Slash Three, or I'll lease it out, or sell it. The only way I can see where you'd have the time would be for us to run everything together and split the profits according to investment. Now, don't look at me that way, Bart Tyler!"

He kept looking at her, a smile breaking on his lips.

45

River of Gold

The year 1952 was a busy one for Giff Cheshire. He wrote and sold a total of twenty-two stories of varying lengths, mostly to the magazine market. "Ridge Runner", a short novel, was sold to *Blue Book*, published by McCall's, the same company that published *Red Book* and *McCall's Magazine*. The next year Cheshire would expand this short novel to form the book-length *Ridge Runner* (Fawcett Gold Medal, 1953) published under the pseudonym Chad Merriman. "River of Gold" must have been written sometime between late May and early June, 1952. It was sold to Alladin Press as the basis for an illustrated book for $500, but for some reason that is not clear the publisher did not bring it out until 1955, three years later. Cheshire said at the time that he was inspired to write this short novel because he hoped it would be the kind of story his teenage children, son Craig and daughter Crete, might want to read. In the event, neither of them did read it . . . not then . . . but eventually they did, once they were adults.

I

The schooner lay before the town, almost hiding the few stores and cabins set on the river's edge. Portland, the place had been named. But upriver, where Boone Rourke lived, the settlement was called Stumptown, because of the torn edge of timber rising sharply along the hills. The land flattened at the waterside where the schooner was tied up to a great sprawling oak tree. She was the *Honolulu* and had made the trip around the Horn to Oregon twice before. News of her arrival had come quickly to Oregon City and Boone had been on the road before dawn with his pack train.

The six pack horses, following slowly after Boone's lead horse, carried loads of flour to be exchanged for the goods Frank Lord needed to sell in his store. The boy had traveled up the narrow east bank trail and now he would have to wait for the ferry to take him across the river.

Boone had a reason of his own for not using the more convenient west bank trail, crossing below the falls at Linnton, a reason bearing the name of Duke Stagg. Duke packed for Moss Hartman, the storekeeper at Linnton. Stagg was a big, burly man, ten years older than Boone and twice his size.

On the last trip Boone had made to meet a ship at Stumptown, Stagg had made his life miserable. Where the trail from Linnton was narrow, he had pressed ahead to crowd Boone's horses, almost pushing one over a cliff. When Boone let the man's pack train pass to avoid a fight, Stagg had waited around a bend and shouted at the horses. He had stood there, leaning against a tree, while Boone tried to quiet the frightened animals.

"Tell Frank Lord not to send a baby face out with a pack train." Stagg's voice still echoed in Boone's ears. And there hadn't been anything he could do about the taunt. A fifteen-year-old boy couldn't fight a man like Stagg. Besides, Frank Lord's bags of flour had to be protected. If the bags had broken open or fallen into the river, there'd have been nothing to trade with.

After this miserable experience Boone decided to play safe and come up the longer, harder trail out of Stagg's reach. In mid-morning he had caught sight, across the river, of Stagg and a companion driving Hartman's pack. They would get to the schooner ahead of Boone and have first pick of the trading goods. They'd be on their way back to Linnton before Boone crossed on the ferry. Then he could do his trading in peace and get the goods home without trouble.

"Have you seen many pack trains from down that way?" he asked the ferryman, as the barge swung out into the river. "From Linnton?"

"Right smart number from upriver and down," the ferryman answered. "Immigrant trains'll be comin' soon. The storekeepers are gettin' ready. Buyin' up everything they can get this year . . . the few that have money. The rest, like you, takin' goods for their wheat. Warehouses crammed. I hear more than two thousand settlers have come across this summer. Of course, a lot will stay at Marcus Whitman's settlement, but plenty will come to us. And the storekeepers are sure gettin' goods to sell 'em."

Boone frowned. Suppose, coming the long trail, he had lost his chance to get the things Frank Lord had needed! Even so, he wouldn't tell the Lords why he had been slow in getting to Portland. He hadn't told them how Duke Stagg bothered him before and he wasn't going to tell them now.

The Lords had been so good to him that he couldn't let them know about Stagg. Mary Lord would say right away it wasn't safe for him to be sent with the pack train, and young Jenny would worry and fret every time he was sent on the road. That girl worried more than a wet hen!

The ferry was nearing shore now. Boone began lining up the horses, getting them into position to make for land as soon as the boatman pulled onto the mud flats.

"If you don't have another trip to make right away, you could just wait for me," Boone said, as he pulled out a coin to pay his fare. There wasn't much money in the settlement but the ferryman had to be paid in hard money. He demanded coin for pay and everybody who had need to ride the ferry saved hard money for the purpose. Between themselves and for schooner trade, barter was the rule.

The ferryman pocketed the coin. Then he shook his head.

"You'll have to go home on the west bank trail, son. This here's my last trip today and for several days to come. I'm goin' on to Butteville to a wedding . . . my own," the man added with a sudden sheepish grin.

But Boone had no answering smile. His only thought was that he was not going to escape Duke Stagg, after all. Somewhere along the way home, he'd meet Moss Hartman's pack train and run into taunting words or maybe a fight he'd be sure to lose.

Gloomily Boone led the patient horses toward the towering hull of the schooner. He was about to hail the ship when he noticed that the captain was at the landing, directing two sailors who were loading sacks of grain.

Wagon wheels creaked as the departing trader made his way inland. A farmer, Boone guessed, and one from a settlement up north where there was no grist mill. At least he'd

50

traded with freshly threshed wheat. Boone's load was good, milled flour.

"What can I do for you?" Captain Newall asked, when the rowboat had pulled away with its load. "Aren't you Frank Lord's pack boy?"

Boone nodded and fished out the list of tools and farm supplies, of pots and pans and yard goods Frank Lord needed. "Here's the list," Boone said, "and here's the flour for trading. Mister Lord hopes you'll give him a good price, sir. Enough to cover his needs. New immigrants will be coming overland soon, and. . . ."

The captain interrupted with a grim laugh. "More than overland wagon trains will be heading for Oregon," he said in his clipped Yankee speech. "I brought a half dozen Californians on my ship, and more will be pouring in from the country to the south. I bet you haven't heard. The Mexican governor has closed California to foreigners!"

"Foreigners?" Boone frowned. "Does that mean Americans? Even Captain Frémont?"

To most Oregon settlers, the young American Army captain was the most important man in California. He was the link that connected them with the land to the south. Frémont had opened the Oregon Trail over the Rockies and then had gone exploring for a trail to California, too, even though that country was foreign soil.

"Captain Frémont's the main one they're after, I reckon," Newall answered. "They ordered him out of Monterey a few months ago and he started for Oregon with his soldiers. Got as far as Klamath Lake, I'm told. Then he got some sort of message from his father-in-law, Senator Benton, back in Washington. Don't know what it said, but it sent Frémont hightailing it to Marysville, in the Sacramento Valley. He gathered up some American settlers that didn't like being

51

sent from their homes. I hear they've raised up a flag . . . the Bear Flag . . . and claimed independence."

"Same as Oregon settlers did at Champoeg?" Boone asked.

"I believe they did point to Champoeg as an example. Champoeg, and Texas. But the Bear Flag won't last. A United States warship came in just before I hoisted anchor and claimed California for the United States. They could do it because Mexico and the United States are at war. Anyhow, it's all a mess down south. I'm not stopping there any more. Hereafter, the *Honolulu* will do its trading between Boston and Portland. But I'm talking too long. Unload your flour and give me that list. You go find yourself something to eat and I'll have your goods ready by the time you get your fill."

Boone glanced nervously toward the main street, up on the hill. Wagons and pack horses stood hitched beside the hotel, and loungers sprawled against door fronts. Although he didn't see any sign of Moss Hartman's pack train, he wasn't taking any chances of meeting Duke Stagg in the hotel dining room. Anyway, Jenny had fixed him a lunch of bread and cold roast pig.

"I'll just wait here," he answered. "Soon as you get back from the ship with my goods, I've got to be starting home."

The way home led through farms, set far apart and lonely. Boone could tell the farms of last year's settlers by the sound of hammers. Now that the wheat harvest was gathered, they were adding rooms to the makeshift huts put up the first winter.

Soon a new stream of immigrants would be arriving, opening new fields, cutting down trees for hurried shelter. Over the evening meal they'd talk about the fields of golden wheat they'd plant come spring. That's the way it would have been with his own family, Boone thought with sudden, heavy loneliness. If only. . . .

The Rourkes had sold their belongings in Missouri in the spring of 1844, when Boone was ten. They had sold out suddenly after Boone's father heard Marcus Whitman speak at the church one evening. Mostly the famous missionary had talked about the Indians. He was on his way back from Boston where he had gone to beg money for his mission. However, while Whitman talked, his hearers caught a vision of the wonderful, sunlit land to be had in the far West, had for the asking, a vision of heaven on earth in the Oregon country.

Boone's father was a schoolteacher, not a farmer. However, afire with this vision, he sold his house, his books, his grandfather clock, and even the big silver watch out of his pocket. With the money, he bought a team of oxen and a wagon with a canvas cover, so the family could set out for Oregon, with Marcus Whitman to lead them.

Independence was the meeting place for the wagon train going West. People had been coming in from all parts of the country—from Boston, like the Lords, from Illinois, from Kentucky. But the Rourkes already lived in Independence. They had lived there even before Boone was born. They had only to close the door of the house that was no longer theirs, and make one last visit to the graveyard where Boone's brother and sister were buried. Then they were ready to climb into their shining new wagon and join the wagon train.

What a mess of horses and oxen and cattle and shouting children on that camping ground! What sweet-smelling smoke from all the cook fires! What calling back and forth and singing.

The first three months of the journey had been wonderful. Boone and his mother had taken turns driving the oxen. His father had been chosen one of the guards to walk ahead across the prairie, across the deserts, across the mountain ranges. Three months, and every day an adventure to Boone, every evening as good as Halloween, with bonfires and ball games and the endless talk of what it would be like in Oregon, about the house they'd build, the wheat they'd grow, the golden wheat.

In September they had come to Marcus Whitman's mission on the Walla Walla River. Some of the families had stayed there in the valley, but the Rourkes and the Lords, who had become their friends on the journey, and about two hundred more were for going farther. The land, they heard, was even better near the coast, and, anyway, the Lords were going to Oregon City to open a store. Frank Lord had been a storekeeper back in Boston and had carried a stock of goods all across the country.

The easy way to finish the journey was down the Columbia River on flatboats manned by Indians, but there were too many travelers and not enough boats. Winter was coming on. The immigrants counted the days that would be left for building shelters before winter.

Ten of the families decided to take an overland trail across one more mountain range to a little river. They were told that the river could be forded if they could beat the rains. But they didn't beat the rains. The trail was very steep and narrow and there was no grass, so the cattle died. Wagon wheels broke and had to be mended. Within sight of the narrow river, the travelers were halted by a cliff. The clumsy wagons had to be lowered, one by one, by ropes in the sweeping rain, and the river at high water could no longer be forded. A raft had to be built—slow work for the shopkeepers and schoolmasters who knew so little of building.

There were no more games at night, no more singing. Hardly a fire could be kept alive in the constant rain. Even so, in spite of all this, the people had kept up their courage, Boone's mother most of all. She spent the evening hours planning aloud, always planning their house, their new life that lay ahead.

The raft was finished, and over and over again the crossing was made. Nine families crossed in safety. Only Boone's parents met with disaster. There was a crash, a splintering of wood against wood, and Boone found himself engulfed in the wild river. When he came to, hours later, Mary Lord told him that his parents had been drowned.

"You'll stay with us, Boone. Jenny will have a playmate, a brother her own age," Mary Lord said, while her husband nodded agreement.

They had put it kindly, but Boone had understood. He had no family. He was an orphan with his own way to make. All the kindness in the world couldn't hide that fact.

Boone shut out the memory abruptly as you would slam a door. At least he could work for his board and be as little trouble as possible. Like, for instance, not complaining about Duke Stagg.

The trail had narrowed now. The farms were left behind. A stretch of uncleared forest lay between Boone and the ford at Linnton. He had passed very few travelers on the road— one or two on foot, a couple in wagons. Suddenly, rounding a bend, he caught sight of Hartman's pack train. The horses were aimlessly rooting for grass. Duke Stagg and his companion were nowhere to be seen. Boone's heart missed a beat. Were they merely giving their horses a rest? Or were they lying in wait for him? The animals almost blocked the way, but there was nothing Boone could do but push on.

A minute later a rock flashed by his head and bounced against a tree across the trail. Boone swallowed his rage and dug his heels into his horse's flank. Another rock! This time the horse was struck in the flank.

Boone pulled up, flung himself out of the saddle as Stagg came from behind a tree trunk.

"Hello, baby face. What've you got your fists doubled up for? You weren't thinking of trying to fight, were you?" Stagg's voice was harsh as a grater.

Forgetting caution, Boone lunged. The lanky figure of Stagg's friend, Spade Hawkins, appeared from nowhere.

"Look at 'im," Stagg said. "The pride of Oregon City!"

Blindly Boone struck the empty air as Stagg stepped aside. Hawkins let out a guffaw.

Suddenly, another voice broke through the harsh laughter. A giant of a man, loose-limbed, black-haired, slipped between Boone and his tormentors.

"Two grown men fighting a lad, is it? Sure, if you're spoiling for a fight, it's Mike Trahan will give it to you. But first," the stranger said easily, "I'll take my coat off. I'll not be ruining a good broadcloth coat on the likes of you."

"Aw, we didn't mean nothin'." Stagg's voice had dropped to a mumble. "Just breakin' in a fresh pack boy from Oregon City. Got to keep him in his place."

Spade Hawkins had already seized his horse's rein and mounted. Now Stagg sidled away and whipped his pack train forward.

It was not until they had disappeared down the trail that Boone realized how his knees were trembling. Moments passed before he could trust himself to speak.

"Looked like you might have a little trouble beating both of those bullies at once," the stranger said. "Hope you didn't mind my interfering."

Boone grinned, suddenly at ease. "I didn't have a chance. Just lost my head when that rock hit my horse's flank. Thank you, mister, for getting me out of a bad hole."

"My name's Mike Trahan," the man said. "Do you have this trouble regular?"

"It's nothing much, sir," Boone stammered. "It's just that Moss Hartman's men don't like anybody from Oregon City. Duke Stagg packs for Hartman's store in Linnton, this side of the Clackamas River. I work for Frank Lord in Oregon City. Frank runs a better store, that's all."

Mike Trahan nodded. "I believe in competition but not that kind. Not with rocks for weapons . . . and not two men against a boy. What I can't see is your family sending you out alone with a fight like this going on."

"I'm almost fifteen," Boone answered hurriedly. "And I haven't any family. I'm an orphan. Besides, nobody knows about Stagg and me."

"And you'd rather I didn't mention it in Linnton?"

"Are you a Linnton man, Mister Trahan?" Boone was surprised. Of course, new settlers were coming in every day and he didn't claim to know everybody on both sides of the river. Yet a man like this—so big and handsome and Irish, too, by his speech, could hardly have gone unnoticed. Boone's father had been Irish and there were not too many hereabouts.

"A Linnton man?" Mike Trahan laughed. "Faith, no. Nor likely to be if the citizens of Linnton are like the sample I've just seen. I'm from Ireland, not a year back. I went to Mexico and found the Mexicans busy with a war. Then I traveled up to California in time for the governor to expel all foreigners. I came into Oregon not twenty-four hours since, on the schooner *Honolulu*, looking for something to turn my hand to. I'm a boat builder by trade."

"Boats?" Boone shook his head. "It's a funny thing but we don't have any boats on the river . . . just the ferry and Indian dugouts, and a raft or two below the falls."

"That's what they told me in Portland. I figured that a flatboat on the river above the falls could do a good trade."

"It could, I'm sure it could," Boone said. "Look here, Mister Trahan, what you want to do is to get on one of my horses and cross the ford with me and talk to Frank Lord. He'll know all about river traffic and trading."

"You think I should become an Oregon City man?" Trahan looked at Boone with a twinkle in his eye.

"It's the fastest growing town in Oregon," Boone answered stoutly. "We've got five hundred people and a newspaper. And if we get to be a United States Territory, we'll have the capital, too."

II

"So that's Oregon City!" Mike Trahan shouted above the roar of the falls. "Snug as a hen on its nest. I like the looks of it."

Boone turned in the saddle and gave the big man astride a pack horse a grateful look. The town did look pretty, in the dusk, with the lamps all lit in the windows. He headed the pack train away from the river road and toward Frank Lord's store.

Usually Boone brought his pack string to the back of the store to unload. Now, because of Mike Trahan, he led the way to the front door. When the storekeeper saw them coming, a concerned look crossed his face.

"Something wrong, Boone?" he asked.

"No. I'll take the horses around later. I've brought a new settler!" He motioned Mike inside the store. "Mister Mike Trahan, from Ireland. He's going to build a flatboat, above the falls, for river trading. I told him he'd do better on our side of the river."

Mike Trahan stepped forward to shake Frank Lord's outstretched hand. His shrewd eyes studied the heavy-set man with thick hair, turned gray at the temples. He was attracted at once to the storekeeper's kindly face, so surprisingly clean-shaven in a country where everybody seemed to wear beards.

"You are welcome," Frank Lord said. "You met Boone on the road?"

"That I did," Trahan answered. "And well met . . . he

saved me from becoming a citizen of Linnton."

Boone was relieved when he saw that his new friend did not mean to mention Duke Stagg.

"I was just about to close up," the storekeeper said. "Boone, you unload and turn the horses into the corral. I'll walk Mister Trahan up to the house." Almost as an afterthought, he turned to the Irishman. "You'll eat with us, I hope? My wife and Jenny will have supper ready."

"Can I be after refusing?" Trahan answered. "It's been a year since I've had a home-cooked meal."

Boone slipped into his place at the supper table. Mike Trahan's booming voice filled the large, pleasant kitchen. The man's plate, piled high with food, was almost untouched. He was too busy answering Mrs. Lord's and Jenny's questions about his trip through Mexico, the voyage up the western coast, and then to San Francisco.

"As wild a settlement as you could hope to see . . . that's San Francisco! The sandy hills come down to the fine big harbor and houses perch on top like feathers on a lady's bonnet. Sure, and a goat can hardly climb up to the rough cabin they call the hotel . . . and when you be getting there 'tis more foreign talk you hear than at the Tower of Babel . . . Spanish, Chinese, Russian . . . to say nothing of Indian, and a word or two of American. The ships come in from every country in the world, attracted by the chance for trading. But now, with Governor Castro expelling the foreigners, it's precious little trade San Francisco will get, I'm thinking."

"Captain Newall says the trade will come to Oregon," Boone said.

"Of course, it will," Jenny Lord agreed. Her dark eyes shone, and her black braids bobbed as she nodded eagerly. You'd think Oregon was something the girl had made with

60

her own hands, to see her pride in it.

"That's what I'm thinking," Mike Trahan answered. "And the quicker the better." He leaned over toward Boone. "Frank has told me just the place to build . . . above the falls and near the sawmill. He says he can spare you one or two days a week, for building, and afterward for going with me on the river, Boone, my boy. How would you like that? It'll be a fair change from packing, eh?"

Boone gulped. It was a fine offer and a chance to make some money of his own. It was true Frank Lord had no need of all his time, but to go on the river. . . . When he was younger, back in Missouri, he'd done a lot of swimming and boating with his father. But not here—not in Oregon, not after that raft overturned and his parents drowned. Ever since then, a river had seemed full of terrors. But he could not explain that to Mike Trahan, nor yet to the Lords, who were giving him this chance to better himself. Even if the river were a thousand times more frightening than Duke Stagg's torments, he'd not let on.

"Sure, Mister Trahan," Boone said. "I'll help with the boat, whenever Frank can spare me from the store."

Within a week, Mike Trahan had thrown up a shack to live in, right at the river front. He had built a landing and a rough tool shed, too, and bought piles of seasoned lumber. The sharp, sweet sound of a hammer came to Boone's ears long before he reached the top of the steep path leading from Oregon City to Canemah Hill. Trahan had found helpers from the Indians living around the falls, and the building of the boat was going forward with great speed and little talk. The Indians understood only a few English words and the Irishman was directing them mostly with signs and gestures.

On this first day that he came to work Boone found him-

61

self a hammer and took his place alongside the Indians, nailing the big square timbers of hardwood. The hull seemed long—longer than its thirty feet. It was about ten feet wide and would rise about three or four feet above the surface of the river, when finished.

Boone wondered if it would have a cabin like the arks and barges he used to see at Independence, Missouri. Whole families lived in those arks. Smoke would pour out of the cookstove chimneys. Clothes would flap on a clothesline aboard the floating homes. Chickens and cows would be neatly fenced in beside the boatman, with his long pole or paddle.

There had even been a store boat that drew up once or twice a year at Independence. Boone remembered the blast of its horn heard long before the boat pulled up to the wharf. At the sound of the storekeeper's horn, the women, with children tagging after them, would hurry to the landing, to buy from the well-filled shelves of the floating store. Boone recalled the dry goods, hardware, big, colored handkerchiefs, and a wonderful jumping-jack his mother had bought him, once, for Christmas.

"We won't be having anything fancy like that," Trahan said when Boone told him about the store boat. "But I'm thinking a horn's not a bad thing for calling the settlers to bring their wheat down . . . and their potatoes. Faith, we'll get hold of a cow's horn and you can blow it."

III

At the Lords', Boone's first chore, each day, was to go to the barn and corral at the edge of town to pump water for the pack horses. Then he'd measure out their oats and fork down some hay. When there was a pack trip to be made, he would halter the animals and put on the wooden saddles, letting the ponies eat, while he went home for his own breakfast.

On a morning, early in September, Jenny had already eaten when Boone returned from the corral. As he passed the store on his way to breakfast, she halted him.

"I'm tidying up early for Pa. He says I can go with you as far as the Mooreheads'."

An hour later, Boone was riding with Jenny up the rough road along the Clackamas River. This had been one of the first sections to be settled and there were several homesteads to be visited as they turned east across the yellow flat, with its brown knolls and fir-greened hills. The saddlebags of the pack horses were, one by one, emptied of pots and pans and shovels and dress goods that had been ordered. They now bulged heavily with wheat and vegetables and smoked meat, taken in exchange.

Jenny's saddlebags were crammed with things Frank and Mary Lord wanted to send the Moorehead children. Although the Mooreheads were among the first settlers, they had not prospered. Hattie Moorehead worked hard enough, and so, in his awkward way, did Ollie, her husband. But Ollie was no farmer. They owed a big bill at the store and even in this year, when Oregon had bumper crops, their harvest was not big enough to pay out. Frank Lord had worried when they sent no order in for goods to be delivered before the winter. "Tell Hattie not to stew about the store bill," he had said, as he packed the saddlebags. "Their credit is good and, if there's anything more they need, tell her to let me know."

Jenny talked about the Mooreheads now as they rode along in the clear warm noontide.

"Ollie's a dreamer," she said. "Hattie told me that he really came out intending to teach at the Indian Mission with Marcus Whitman and old Doctor Appleton, Hattie's father. Then he met Hattie . . . and they got married, and then with all the children. . . ."

Boone laughed. "I guess Ollie had to go to farming, just to feed five young 'uns." Laughing came easily to Boone today, out here in the sun-drenched countryside, riding with Jenny beside him.

There were no homes in sight now, only the wild, grassy knolls and the shining green timber. The land must have looked just this way in the far past at the beginning of the century, when explorers had made their daring journey across the continent. But even the explorers had not expected so many people would follow them over the mountains. Three thousand new settlers, the newspaper at Oregon City had predicted for this autumn.

Boone and Jenny had not much longer to ride before the log buildings on the Moorehead claim rose before them in the distance. First the barn and smokehouse, then the three-sided shed, and finally the dog-trot cabin came into sight. By the time Boone and Jenny rode up to the place, the yard was full of children and dogs. Hattie Moorehead, broad-hipped and golden-haired, waved from the cabin doorway.

"Why, bless you!" she cried.

Laughing and surrounded by the children, the visitors swung down from their saddles. Jenny opened the saddlebags and pulled out the presents: new shoes for the boys and dress goods for the girls. And for Hattie, a new tin pie pan. At the very bottom of the bag was Ollie's present—a book of poems by Henry Wadsworth Longfellow, wrapped for safekeeping in a copy of the *Oregon Spectator*. Frank Lord had taken the book in trade from one of the farmer's wives and he'd said at once that Ollie Moorehead should have it.

"Where's Ollie?" Boone asked.

"He's down trying to fix our fence again. We're always having to run the cows out of the wheat and even out of my garden."

A "worm fence" separated the crop fields and stock pasture. The top rails were held together with rawhide strips that were forever getting loosened. Then the animals could push down the rails and get into the wheat.

"I'll go down and help him," Boone said.

Hattie shook her head. "No, you don't. It's dinnertime and I was just about to send Pat to fetch his father."

"Can I carry the book down to show Pa?" five-year-old Pat asked. "And can I wear my new shoes?"

"Neither one nor the other," his mother said firmly. "Those shoes are not for scratching through the fields. And as for the book! Once your father laid eyes on it, he'd not appear till nighttime. You just tell him Boone and Jenny are here. That'll fetch him quicker'n anything."

As Pat ran off across the yard, Hattie turned to the visitors. "You go water your horses, Boone, and Jenny'll come with me to lay two more places on the table. One of you will have to eat out of the new pie pan."

"We don't want to make any trouble for you . . . ," Jenny began.

"Trouble! You're as welcome as sunshine after rain!" cried Hattie. "And there are enough vegetables in the garden to feed an immigrant train." She sighed lightly. "If it weren't so hard to get things to market, the Mooreheads would make out pretty well this year. I've been drying a lot of peas and done some canning, too, and the wheat's all cut. It's a pity Ollie hasn't got it threshed yet. He could have sent it to the mill by Boone."

It was too bad, Boone thought, as he pumped water for the horses into the wooden trough. Ollie would have a day's trip to the flour mill. With just one horse to carry the wheat, that meant several trips and many days lost, that were needed on the farm. Maybe it wasn't all Ollie's fault that the Mooreheads hadn't made out as well as they ought to. Maybe other farmers had the same problem, too. And maybe Mike Trahan was on the way to solving it.

"How far are you from the river, Ollie?" he asked a little abruptly, when they were all crowded together around the dinner table.

"Straight west and going cross-country not more'n an hour," Ollie answered. He had to raise his voice to make himself heard above the clatter of dishes being passed back and forth.

"That's it!" Boone cried, and told about the trading boat Mike Trahan was building. "You get the neighbors together and build a landing," he said. "Mister Trahan will have his boat launched in a little while now. He'll bring your wheat to town."

"I've got you a customer!" Boone called next morning, as he came over Canemah Hill to Trahan's shack. But there was no answering shout from the Irishman. He was leaning against the doorframe, discouragement in every sagging muscle. His face, usually so quick to show a smile, was drawn and grim.

"Customers, in faith," Trahan said bitterly. "What are they without a flatboat?"

"Something's happened to the boat?"

"She was sunk in the night," Trahan continued quietly. "I should have left a guard, I suppose, with the craft so near launching . . . and knowing Hartman was watching me from across the river. I knew the man didn't like competition, but I never thought he would fight dirty like that in a fair, big land where there's room for all to live."

"You think Moss Hartman sank your boat?" Boone could scarcely believe it.

"Who else would come across the river in the night and bore holes with an auger? Crazy, trusting fool that I am! I heard the water lapping soft like . . . thought it was some animal swimming across. Even heard the grinding sound of the awl. 'Beaver,' I said to myself, half asleep. Then suddenly I woke myself and ran outside in time to see the water coming up in the boat and the shadow of a rowboat being pulled up on the far bank across the river. Out of range of my gun," Trahan added bitterly.

"You're sure it was Hartman's doing? Could it have been the Indians?"

Trahan shook his head. "I can't prove anything," he said. "But it wasn't my Indians. They came to work at dawn the same as always. I've sent 'em off to get some help, to see if we can raise the boat. They went, as low in spirit as myself, I'm thinking."

"Even if you can raise it, the delay will give Hartman a head start with his pack trains," Boone muttered. "Now he'll go to the river towns and he'll take the trade to Linnton. He's . . . he's bad." Boone clenched his fist and tears came to his eyes.

The sight of the boy's anger somewhat soothed Trahan's own. He straightened up and the black look left his face. In its place came a look of determination, of courage.

"There's bad and there's good, and we have to take both, lad. This is not the end of things. It's just a hard beginning."

Boone wouldn't have thought it possible that he'd have no time at all to help with raising and repairing Mike Trahan's flatboat, but it happened that on the day he heard the news of the sinking, the first wagon train of immigrants came over the trail. From that moment, until the winter rains set in, neither the Lords nor Boone had a minute to spare. The store was crowded from morning to night with newcomers wanting to buy tools and building supplies, and food to last them until they could raise a crop.

When he wasn't waiting on customers, Boone was off on hurried pack train trips to Stumptown to meet a schooner to get more things to sell. At night, over supper, there was news to talk over. Jenny seemed to have a special knack of gathering news from the immigrants, as she weighed up bacon or sugar for their needs. She was better than the *Spectator* in collecting bits and pieces of information about affairs back East, and she patched the bits together as deftly as she would a patchwork bedcover.

"The boundary between Canada and Oregon has all been settled, but Congress is still delaying about making Oregon a territory," she reported one evening. "A woman from New York told me that the lawmakers are still haggling over the one last point. Some don't like the part in our Provisional

Government Constitution that says Oregon shall be free of slavery."

"As if we'd consider making slaves of other human beings, black or white!" Mary Lord exclaimed, banging the lid on the stove.

The stove was Mrs. Lord's great pride. Most of the other families in Oregon City still had to cook on open fireplaces. For her to handle the stove roughly showed how strongly she felt about slavery.

That's because the Lords come from Boston, Boone. thought. In Missouri, where he'd come from, some people believed in having slaves and some didn't. In Massachusetts, everyone thought slavery was wrong. Living with the Lords, Boone had come to believe that, too.

"Of course, Oregon won't come into the Union other than as a free state," he said. "Not California, either, if it gets to be part of America."

"The immigrants think Captain Frémont will be the governor in California," Jenny reported.

Another evening she announced that, if the United States won the war, they'd have all the land between the Río Grande and Oregon. "The man I sold the plow to told me. The government is going to get every bit of the land. Even where the Mormons have settled in Salt Lake."

"That won't keep the immigrants from coming to Oregon," Frank Lord said. "The Mexican land, California included, is nothing but mountains and deserts. It's here the people will find land to grow wheat."

Three separate immigrant trains made their way to Oregon that summer—the full three thousand that had been expected. Over five hundred of these came to the neighborhood of Oregon City, doubling the population.

More of the newcomers had come to the coast than had

stayed at Walla Walla this year, and for a disturbing reason. The Indians, who had been so friendly with Marcus Whitman and the other missionaries in the Walla Walla Valley, had changed. There was even talk that violence might be expected. It had started with the killing of Elijah, son of one of the chiefs. His father was demanding that the murder be punished. Although the killers couldn't be found, the chief still demanded punishment. One immigrant said that Dr. Marcus Whitman's own life had been threatened. Another explained that it was not Elijah's killing, alone, that was causing the trouble. There had been much sickness and many deaths among children treated at the mission. The Indians claimed that the white men were poisoning their children.

This tale upset Hattie Moorehead when she heard it. She had come down to the store one day in December to do a little Christmas shopping, and Jenny had poured out the story. However, when she saw the sad look that crossed the older woman's face, she wished she'd kept this news to herself. She had forgotten that Hattie's father, old Dr. Appleton, was one of the missionaries at Walla Walla.

It was not so much the fear of anything happening to her father that disturbed Hattie, as the misunderstanding between the white men and the Indians. Then, too, she mourned the death of the Indian, Elijah. She had known him well. Her father had taught him English and he had been in their home often—a fine, upstanding, educated young man. Not a man to be killed by ignorant traders. As for the Indians thinking the doctors at the mission had poisoned the children—that mistrust was an old one. It came, Hattie said, from the fact that the Indians could not understand white men's diseases.

"When we lived at the mission," she explained, "before we took up our land claim, there was an outbreak of measles. My children and some of the Indian children came down with it. Doctor Whitman treated all alike, all with the same medicine. My children got well of the measles. The Indian children died. You can see how that would make the Indians feel."

It was almost dark when Hattie Moorehead was ready to start for home. Boone and Jenny rode to the edge of town with her and Boone offered to ride all the way along the lonely trail.

"Lonely?" Hattie laughed. "With all the new settlers that have come in this fall? There's scarcely a moment I'll be out of sight of the light from a farmhouse. Lamps in fresh-cut windows, cook fires of those still living in tents . . . oh, it's a fine thing to see the lights of homes numerous as the stars. A fine thing to me, who knew Oregon in its emptiness."

"Numerous as stars," Jenny repeated softly, as they watched Hattie ride away. "Think of what it'll be when all these new settlers plant their wheat next year!"

The weather had turned wet and dreary. Great winds howled across the valley. Roads were soon impassable to anything on wheels. Sheets of brown water stopped all but foot and horseback travel. Creeks began to pour their swollen discharge into the river, and the river was out of its banks.

On Christmas morning, the Lords had a surprise visitor. Mike Trahan walked in, looking like a real frontiersman in fur cap and boots and leather clothes. Over his shoulder, wrapped in a gunny sack, he carried a big salmon he had got from the Indians.

"The boat's launched!" he boomed, as soon as Christmas greetings were over. "When the weather breaks, I'm going to make a trip. I wanted to know if I could borrow Boone to come along with me. We'll go all the way to the Yamhill towns."

71

"Just you and Boone?" Mrs. Lord asked, a little anxiously.

Trahan shook his head. "I've got boatmen . . . Indians who are used to handling canoes and the big *bateaux* of the fur traders, but I need Boone, too, if you can spare him. And a stock of goods, as well."

Swept along by Trahan's enthusiasm, Boone forgot he hated water travel. The Lords were filled with excitement, too.

Jenny's eyes flashed. "You'll go all the way up the Yamhill River? That will show Moss Hartman!"

Hartman's pack trains had made a few trips beyond Portland but the trail did not extend as far as the Yamhill Valley. The Yamhill settlers were served neither by pack train nor by water.

"I can spare Boone," Frank Lord said. "It's a great chance for the boy and good business for me, besides. We'll not be too rushed again here at the store until the new crops begin coming in . . . and the ships from the East. Eighteen Forty-Eight should be a great year for Oregon."

"A great year," the Irishman agreed.

IV

The Indian oarsmen were already in place when Boone came in sight of Mike's boat at Canemah Landing. There was a sail to be used when the wind was right, sparing the oarsmen. Aboard, also, was a shipment of freight for the town of La Fayette, and Boone had brought a load of goods from the store.

Although Trahan was unusually quiet, his black eyes danced. It was clear that he considered it a great occasion. "The top of the morning to you, lad! Are you ready to go exploring?"

The morning grew bright and fine. Willow and alder hugged the banks. Their branches, newly clothed in green, overhung the twisting, slate-green of the river. Beyond, the country stepped back in a series of forested hills.

Trahan's goal was the new towns around the falls of the Yamhill River. The valley of that river ran deeply to the westward Coast Mountains. Its oak-studded bottomland and timbered hills were of the best. Its earlier settler had been Ewen Young, who took land near the Chehalem Mountains while the country was still ruled by Hudson's Bay Company. With some other settlers, he had brought six hundred head of Spanish longhorns up from California, to start Oregon's first herds of cattle.

The flatboat passed the mouth of the Tualatin River under sail, then the upthrusts of Rock Island. The brush and hugging hills began to fall back, but the high, overgrown banks of the Clackamas River still shut off far views.

Boone did not know the country they were entering now, but he knew that east and south lay the great reach of Mission Bottom, with the earlier-settled French Prairie beyond. On the other side of the river, the Chehalem country began to wheel in. They passed the ferry in late day and tied up for the night a little above the ferry landing, camping on the river-bank where it was carpeted with trillium flowers.

The next morning they moved past the towns of Butteville and Champoeg without putting in to land. Trahan said they'd get to them on the way back. When they came at last to the mouth of the Yamhill River, Trahan ordered the sail furled. The rapids ahead would have to be run by the oarsmen and it would be heavy work.

At last they came in below the rapid just down the Yamhill from La Fayette. Trahan was grinning, and Boone saw why. A crowd waited for them, the late sun at its back.

"Word seems to travel faster than our boat," Trahan said. "I wonder how they knew we were coming."

"Maybe the ferryman told somebody who crossed the river," Boone guessed, thinking of the settlement's grapevine system of communication.

"Could it be that Frank got word to La Fayette that it will soon have river trade?"

"Might have," Boone agreed.

The flatboat put in to the bank, tied up, and unloaded quickly. Bags of wheat were soon exchanged for hardware and farm tools and seeds. The shipment of freight was claimed by one of the stores.

"And now, lads," Trahan said to the onlookers, "you've seen it done right handily. I hope to make this a regular thing. I'll haul down your wheat to the grist mill and bring you whatever you need."

A man had his thumbs stuck under his belt with a swaggering look on his bearded face.

"We're glad enough to have boat service," he said, "but you'd better get some different boatmen. We don't like Indians around here . . . not after the news from the Walla Walla."

"What news?" Boone put in hurriedly.

The man stared. "You mean you haven't heard about the massacre? Marcus Whitman and twelve others killed in cold blood! Fifty more settlers barely rescued by the Hudson's Bay people. I tell you, if the United States government doesn't do something to protect us, we'll give the country back to Britain!"

"Marcus Whitman dead by violence?" Mike Trahan looked grave. "I've heard he was a good man."

"Good as they come," the man muttered. "Old Doctor Appleton, too. Always putting themselves out for the redskins. Only way to meet 'em, I say, is with a gun."

Dr. Appleton! Poor Hattie . . . Boone wondered if she'd heard. He was too moved to speak.

But Trahan had hot words on his tongue and was quick to answer the La Fayette man.

"There's good and there's bad among every people. I'll not be blaming all Indians for the evil done by a few. I grieve for the good men killed at the mission but I've seen the bones of red men, too, whitening in the sun. Come on, Boone," he ordered, "get the wheat aboard. We'll go above the rapids before we stop for the night."

A few La Fayette settlers helped load the boat but most stood sullenly by, watching the bewildered Indian boatmen. One or two fingered their powder horns and guns.

"Will you go to La Fayette again?" Boone asked, when they were safely afloat midstream.

"Sure, and with my Indian boatmen, too," Trahan answered comfortably. "The massacre at the mission is a grievous thing, but the people of Oregon will not be so crazy as to blame a whole race for the crimes of a few. They'll cool down and come to see that there's wrong and right on both sides."

"But Doctor Whitman and Doctor Appleton were good men."

"I know, Boone," the Irishman said quietly. "They're true martyrs to a cause. You'll learn as you grow older that no great work, like building a country, has ever been accomplished without its martyrs. It's not right. It's not just. But it's the history of mankind."

They dropped back down to the Willamette River to camp for the night. The next day found them riding on the current, the Indians rowing comfortably as the flatboat sped home. In the early evening they tied up at the Canemah Landing.

Before Boone started down the path to Oregon City, Trahan sprang a surprise.

"Frank and I have been talking over your future, Boone. Frank agrees with me that the settlements will have plenty of storekeepers. From now on, it's river men we'll be needing. If you're willing, lad, I'd like to train you to handle a flatboat for me. If things work out, I'll lay down the keel for another boat right soon."

Boone flushed. "You really think I could learn to handle a boat? You . . . you really think there'll be a need?"

"Why not?" Trahan demanded. "Before the summer's out, the riverbanks will be a checkerboard of golden wheat. There'll be a flour mill and warehouse, likely, at La Fayette, and others as far up as the Long Tom River. In the timber belts there'll be sawmills . . . more than one. Faith, and I'm thinking these rivers will soon need heavier ships than flatboats. I could build a steamboat right at my own landing. Do you think you'd like to be a river man?"

The thought came to Boone: *Don't forget it was on the water your parents died.* His throat tightened and his lips felt dry and stiff. And yet, if Mike Trahan and Frank Lord thought he could do it, and if Oregon needed men on the river. . . . "I'd like to try," Boone said slowly.

"Good!" Trahan boomed. "And we'll get that second boat before the year's out, if I prosper!"

Boone divided his time between river trade and packing. In June and July, two schooners and a dipper came into Stumptown harbor from the East, loaded with goods to exchange for timber and flour. This was more ships than had ever come before. The troubled state of California's government and the war between the United States and Mexico led the Yankee traders to give San Francisco a wide berth. California's troubles appeared to be Oregon's good fortune.

Then one day, early in August, Frank Lord heard that the *Honolulu* had put in at Stumptown. He had Boone get the pack train loaded and gave him a long list of goods needed at the store.

Boone crossed at the ford and made his way north as quickly as possible. If Moss Hartman's men gave him trouble, he'd just have to grin and bear their taunts. Besides, he'd grown so much taller and heavier that he felt almost ready to give Duke Stagg a fight. He reached Stumptown without incident, however, and found the rough, dusty street filled with pack animals and their owners.

Something strange was going on. Captain Newall was buying but he was not selling! He was buying everything in sight—not flour and timber, alone, but shovels, picks, crowbars, and other hardware. Storekeepers were bringing down to the landing the very things the trading ships usually brought in. The captain of the *Honolulu* was paying for everything in gold dust.

Captain Newall refused to explain his odd behavior. He seemed anxious to load his ship and get away. The sailors, however, were not so close-lipped. The word leaked out that gold had been found on the American River in California. An Oregon carpenter, Jim Marshall, had found gold while building a sawmill for Captain Sutter. Marshall had sent a letter to his cousin, a blacksmith, to come down by ship to stake out a claim and start digging.

The letter passed from hand to hand. It was in tatters before Boone got a sight of it. Already the blacksmith and a little knot of friends were talking to Newall about taking passage to San Francisco. They stood aside while Boone turned over his flour, getting a pouch full of gold dust in place of the goods Frank Lord needed.

Since there were no more pack trains and the stores of Portland were cleaned out, Captain Newall was suddenly ready to talk.

"I'll take as many passengers as I can," he drawled. "And you won't get another ship soon. It's a mighty big thing, this gold find, with signs that every river coming out of the Sierras is just as rich as the American. The word has gone East already. There'll be a boom down in California such as this world has never seen."

Boone moved away, the pouch in his pocket heavy enough to be uncomfortable. Some of its weight lay on his spirit as well, as he saw five good settlers from Oregon rowing out to the *Honolulu*.

Frank Lord wasn't going to be happy about the day's news either, he thought, as he crossed the river on the ferry—or Mike Trahan. They had put their hopes in building the Oregon settlements. To do this there had to be sea trade and a steady flow of immigrants. Now Captain Newall said the ships wouldn't bother to come any farther than San Francisco, and, instead of new settlers coming in, five were leaving.

In the late afternoon, Boone was driving his pack train with their empty saddlebags through the village of Milwaukie. A woman came out of a store with a little package of coffee.

"Hello, Hattie Moorehead!" Boone called. He had seen her only once since he and Jenny had carried the news of her father's death out to the ranch. He had always liked Hattie but his feeling for her had grown when he saw the courage with which she had weathered that blow. "Is everything all right out your way?" he asked.

Hattie Moorehead smiled. "We make do. The wheat's almost ready to cut. Ollie opened a new field and I've begun keeping bees. We got a ride over here today with one of our new neighbors. I heard there was a settler here from the Walla Walla, and I wanted to talk to him. I still can't believe it, Boone, about Marcus Whitman and my father."

Boone swallowed. "You heard they'd sent to the East to ask the United States for soldiers?"

Hattie Moorehead stared straight ahead. "Peace and friendship cannot be built with guns in the hands of one race to subdue another," she said. "How often have I heard my father and Elijah discuss this! And now both of them are dead by violence."

"Did you find out anything new about the massacre?" Boone asked abruptly.

"I didn't see the man," she answered. "He'd left, bag and baggage, for California this morning."

"This morning!" How fast the news had traveled. "You've

heard why? You've heard about the gold?"

Hattie gestured helplessly toward the store. "Ollie's in there talking about it now," she said.

"I hope he's not thinking of going to dig gold!" Boone burst out. "Not after all the work you've put in on your land!"

"I hope not, Boone," Hattie answered briskly. "Come out to see us, you and Jenny."

"We'll surely do that," Boone promised, and started his horse off with a flick of the reins. He was not sorry to get away before Ollie Moorehead came out. Ollie'd be just the kind to go off searching for gold.

When he came into Oregon City, Boone drove the horses to the corral, watered them, and gave them grain. There was no use going to the store. Frank Lord would already have gone home for supper and there was nothing to unload. Boone walked down the long street to the house, the gold dust still dragging heavily in his pocket.

"Did you get the goods?" Frank asked, as soon as Boone opened the kitchen door.

The family was sitting around the table and the room was fragrant with the smell of Mary Lord's cooking. Boone pulled the heavy, bulging pouch out of his pocket. "That's all I got," he said. The bag of gold dust dropped on the table with a thud.

"What's that?" Frank asked. "I gave you a long list of things to bring up from the trader."

"All I got was gold dust, and Captain Newall says he won't be back. He says no ships will bother coming to Oregon. There's been a big discovery of gold in California and the word's gone East. Captain Newall figures the gold will start a mighty rush of people to California and he's getting ready to make money out of it. And five Oregon settlers have left and I don't know how many more!"

For a minute there was complete silence. Then Mary Lord said firmly: "I don't believe it. They couldn't have left Oregon for that foreign country."

"California's not foreign any more, Ma," Jenny reminded her mother. "The United States' flag is flying over it."

"Somebody's found some gold all right," Frank muttered. "Fool's gold, maybe."

"If it weren't true, why would Captain Newall buy all the picks and shovels?" Boone asked. "Surely not to take them all the way back to the States."

"So that's why Moss Hartman was over here this evening trying to buy my horses." Frank pushed his plate back. His appetite for food was gone. "I thought he'd gone daft. He probably had got wind of this news and wanted to pack a load overland to the gold fields."

Mary Lord's eyes flashed. "Planning to sell his stock at prices no Oregon settlers can pay! What will the immigrants do when they come in next month with no goods to buy . . . no tools, no food?"

"Maybe there won't be any immigrants," Boone answered. He wondered what Mike Trahan would think of this news—with his flatboat trade. "I think I'll hike up the trail after supper and see Mike," he said.

"Mike ought to be told," Mrs. Lord agreed. "And I can send him some of this ham and some cinnamon rolls. The poor man, living up there alone and no one to cook for him!"

It was full dark when Boone came to the end of the rocky trail above the hills. Seated in his doorway, Trahan saw Boone coming and let out a yell so cheerful that Boone guessed he hadn't heard anything.

"Howdy, Boone!" he burst out. "Have you heard the grand news from California?"

81

"Grand news?" Boone gasped.

"A miracle, lad."

"Mike, are you . . . daft?" Boone answered, using Frank Lord's words.

The Irishman roared. "Then you haven't heard!"

"Of course, I heard. I brought the word to Oregon City myself. It's got the Lords down in the mouth, and no wonder. The ships will stop coming here, and so will the wagon trains of immigrants. Why would they come here, with free gold to be had in California?"

"I suppose there's no gold here?" Trahan snorted. "Don't you see, Boone? All those people in California will have to eat. We have our own kind of gold . . . the ripening wheat. Ever since I heard the news, I've been thinking. We'll have the market for our farm products that we've always needed."

Boone had come home cheered from his visit to Trahan. However, when he came down with Frank the next morning to open the store, all his fears returned stronger than ever. From end to end the long street was lined with pack horses, farm wagons, and shouting, excited men.

"Here he comes, finally!" Hans Richter, the millwright, called and the crowd followed Frank to the store like water being poured through a funnel.

Frank Lord had to shoulder his way through a group waiting outside, to get the door unlocked. Boone kept close to his side and the men pressed into the store behind them.

Boone saw that Frank's face was tight, almost frightened. Motioning to Boone, he went on to the back room.

"Know what it means, Boone?" Frank asked when he had shut the door behind them. "They want to outfit for the mines."

"What will you do?" Boone asked.

"I've no right to refuse them. Even if I did, they'd go somewhere else to buy what they want. But I never expected to see so many get their heads turned by gold this quick. Come on. It looks like we'll have a busy day."

Men milled about and called out to be waited on. Presently Frank sent off a boy to bring Mrs. Lord and Jenny down to help. Even the four of them could not keep up with the demands. The gold hunters wanted tools, clothing, blankets, provisions, gunpowder, and caps. A few paid in money for what they bought. Others offered farm produce. Some even asked Frank to wait for his pay until they could send back the gold dust.

A dozen times Boone heard voiced the strong undercurrent of worry in them: "We've got to get down there and stake claims!"

At the end of the day, once the store doors were locked, Frank rubbed a tired hand over his face. "We must have done five hundred dollars' worth of business," he muttered. "I've never seen the like of it."

Mary Lord looked at her husband anxiously. "It means an awful lot of men are leaving us, doesn't it?"

"Too many. Well, I hope we saw the worst of it today."

Boone realized that the first rush was only the beginning. Day after day he and the Lord family worked in the store, selling as fast as they could. New groups of buyers appeared from other settlements until Frank's stock of the kind of thing they needed was all but sold out.

Meanwhile, Boone noticed other changes in the town. The other storekeeper, a young man who had latterly set up in business, had sold his small stock of goods. Then he had locked his door and headed for the mining country himself. Two of the town's doctors had gone and one of its ministers. The grist mill wheel was stilled. Hunsaker's cabinet shop was deserted, an unfinished table standing inside by the window. On Sunday Boone saw mostly women, old men, and children at church.

Then came the moment when Boone glanced up across the counter to see Ollie Moorehead standing before him.

"Ollie!" Boone blinked. "Surely . . . surely you're not going! Ollie, you come with me a minute!" Boone all but pushed Ollie Moorehead into the back room where Frank was hanging some hams.

A look of concern crossed Frank's face. "Man, you can't go off and leave that big family."

"And why not?" Ollie asked defiantly.

"For one thing, I won't outfit you," Frank said.

"Then I'll go across the river to Moss Hartman's," Ollie said, and swung about.

"Wait," Frank said. "How about your wheat? You have it cut?"

"It'll keep."

"Hattie can't harvest it, Ollie."

"Then let it rot. I'll send gold dust back to her before winter. She'll be better off than she's ever been."

"You owe me a big bill already," Frank said, seeking a way to bring his friend to reason.

"And I'll pay it the first thing when I've made my strike." Plainly argument was useless. He was bent on going and would go.

"All right, Ollie," Frank said. "You're your own boss."

Later, Ollie walked out with a loaded pack. Frank looked a long moment at Boone and added: "That's what it's doing to them all. Only, in Ollie it shows up worse."

The rush of business in Lord's store began to slack off. Frank had no more picks and shovels, no more boots or dried foods to sell. However, the departure of settlers and

84

townsmen did not slow up. Men got together what provisions and tools they already had and struck out. The long trail to California had become a rainbow trail, with a pot of gold at the far end.

V

About two weeks after the rush began, Mike Trahan came into the store looking grim. He said: "Frank, have things slowed up enough for you to be letting me have Boone now? I need him. I've lost my boatmen to the mines."

Boone looked up in surprise. He had heard that the Indians were not taking any interest in the gold strike.

"They're not going to dig for gold. They call the stuff bad medicine. They've been hired by a bunch of settlers from above the falls, near Salem, to paddle one of those big French *bateaux*," Mike continued. "I can get some new oarsmen, but they'll not be well-trained. I'm thinking I could use Boone. I want to go to the Yamhill towns now that the harvest is in."

"I can spare Boone," Frank answered. "There's nothing else to sell except women's dress goods and such. And no schooners coming in."

Boone ran to the corral to fetch a couple of horses and packed the saddlebags with what little trading goods Frank had. An hour later he followed Mike up to Canemah Hill.

Early next morning they set out in the flatboat. Boone noticed that Moss Hartman's pack train was gathering across the river. He wondered if they'd meet up with them somewhere upriver.

"Moss sends his packers south with everything he can find to sell at high prices," Trahan said, as he hoisted sail. "Hartman doesn't bother with the river towns any more. The settlers' wheat can go to rot for all he cares. We'll stop at the west bank towns on the way back and bring in the wheat to Oregon City. The farmers will be glad to see us, I'm thinking."

But there were no welcoming crowds at the landing when Boone blew his horn to announce the trade boat's arrival. One or two farmers brought sacks of freshly threshed grain. A sun-bonneted woman or two brought pats of cheese or honeycombs to exchange for cloth. A few of the newly settled immigrants came looking in vain for tools.

For the most part, however, there were few customers. The wheat that should have been threshed and bagged, ready to be made into flour, stood uncut in the fields. Several canoes passed Trahan's boat, making their way to the south. The frail craft were loaded with men setting out for the gold fields.

"They'll have to portage the canoes around the falls," Boone said, "and I'll bet they'll have plenty more portages in the south country. All that work when they could be growing things in the fields they'd cleared!"

"Work and danger, too," Trahan agreed, pointing to a bit of wreckage near the rapids. "Somebody likely lost his life in the greed for easy riches, and it won't be the last one! The effect of gold is to bring famine and death to the fruitful land of Oregon."

At La Fayette a crowd had gathered at the landing and Trahan grew more cheerful at the sight.

"Bring on your wheat men!" he bellowed. "I've come to haul it to market."

A lanky, yellow-bearded man answered: "Not my wheat, mister. I'm going south."

"Then be off with you," Trahan said sullenly.

"And so's everybody here!" a boy, not more than thirteen, shouted. "It's the mines for us, mister, and you can

87

root for your wheat, for all we care."

"Why the hurry, lads?" Trahan asked, drawing close to the landing place.

"We aim to stake our mining claims before people can get there from back East. We're waiting for the raft that's coming to pick us up. We ain't the only ones packing out. I bet there's a hundred others going from this valley alone."

Not until then did Boone see a bit of the light dying in Trahan's black eyes. "You're touched with the sun, the lot of you!" the Irishman shouted defiantly. "Gold's found and spent and that's the end of it. Your land and what it can grow is the Lord's real bounty without end. Stay on your claims, lads, if you want it to go well with you."

"Hear the man!" a burley gray-beard guffawed. "He says it's better to slave and go ragged than to take money right off the ground!"

"The devil take you all then!" Trahan said, as a roar of laughter went up from the crowd. "Get on with you to your mines!"

He motioned to the oarsmen to turn back. When dark came, they tied up for the night, and the next day found them riding on the current. The Indians rowed comfortably; the flatboat speeded home.

There had not been much talk between Boone and Trahan on the return trip. What was there to say?

When he came back to the Lords, however, Boone went straight to Frank.

"If you can spare me again," he said, "I'd better go out to Mooreheads' and help Hattie get in that wheat. It must be more than ripe."

The older man smiled, for the first time in many days. "I figure so, too, Boone. But I wanted you to decide for yourself. Ollie went off and left his wheat standing. He told me it could rot for all of him. But it won't rot. Hattie and the children will get it in somehow. You can be a big help."

Boone rode out to the homestead that evening, spare clothing in his saddlebags because the job at hand would take time. He saw, as he rode in toward the cabin, that the wheat was indeed overripe and that Hattie had already started to cut it.

Anger bit him, although he realized that Ollie had done only what hundreds of other heads of families were doing. They all expected to send home gold dust within weeks and did not consider themselves neglectful.

Mrs. Moorehead was crossing the yard, as he turned in. She cried: "Boone again! What brings you 'way off here at this time of week?"

"Well," Boone said, "things slacked off at the store. So I figured I'd like a taste of country life again, if you don't mind."

"Mind?" She laughed. "Bless you, Boone, I'm happy to have you. But I should warn you, I'm cutting the wheat. You picked a bad time for a vacation."

"I didn't come for a vacation, Hattie," he said. "I came to help."

He slept that night in the loft, with the three young boys, and rose at daylight. But Hattie was up before him.

"I'll milk," Boone said. "I learned to do that back East."

"Remember how?"

"I don't think I'll ever forget."

Hattie gave him pails, and he went to the barn. He milked the two cows, then drove the cows out to the pasture. When he got back, breakfast was ready: boiled wheat with milk to drink. Boone ate with good appetite.

Afterward, he said: "Now, you let me tend to the wheat."

Mrs. Moorehead smiled, flushing a little. "The cradle's

hard for me to handle," she admitted. "If you'll cut, I'll rake and shock."

"All right," Boone said. That would be easier for her than what she had been trying to do all by herself, except as the children could help. He knew that they were not to be left out of account, the two older ones, Elizabeth and Ed, being first-rate at the lighter jobs about the homestead.

Boone fell to work at a job that was to last nearly three weeks. The cradle, with which he moved upon the ripe wheat, had a curling handle that gave it the name: grapevine. On the handle, one above the other, were fingers that caught the grain as it was cut and let him throw it on his left at the end of each swing.

Presently Hattie came out to rake and bind. She bundled the grain, then deftly twisted and tied a band of straw about it. Elizabeth and Ed shocked the bundles she dropped behind her.

By mid-morning the sun was burning hotly overhead. It plagued Boone until late in the afternoon. A good cradler might cut as much as two acres of wheat from sunup to sundown. Boone, without experience, was content with half of that.

Slowly they took in the harvest. Then they were faced with the job of threshing it out. First the shocks were picked up with Ollie's wagon and taken to a stack in the barnyard. They had to be left for a few days, for the straw to sweat, which helped loosen the grain in the hulls. Then the bundles were placed with the heads toward the center of a ring some thirty feet across, and the bands were removed.

Next, the horse was led around and around the ring, trampling the wheat until all the grain came loose and dropped from the hulls. The final step was to carry off the straw so that what was left could be tossed in the wind and the chaff blown away. It was a slow job, but it worked.

It was the end of September before the grain was harvested. The regular chores had absorbed much of Boone's time and there was also the cooking and housework for the Mooreheads. But, rewarding them for the hard labor, the barn at last held nearly two hundred bushels of wheat. The golden grain would bring at least a dollar a bushel. Boone wondered if Ollie had yet earned two hundred dollars in the gold fields.

On the last evening, Boone and Hattie walked through the twilight from the barn to the cabin. Boone said: "I guess I'll go home tomorrow or the next day. Mike Trahan will probably want to try the river again."

"I can't tell you how grateful I am," Hattie said, trying to hide the tiredness in her voice. "Now I feel more like facing the long winter."

"Maybe Ollie will be home before then."

"Maybe. And maybe . . . he'll be rich."

It was late the next afternoon before Boone got away. He decided to check the fences and found repairs he had to make. Afterward, he spent hours splitting a pile of wood for the fireplace. Then at last he rode out, turning back to wave to the children, time and again, until the ground swells finally swallowed the homestead.

Frank had closed the store by the time he reached Oregon City. When he had put up his horse at the corral, Boone walked down the long street toward home. The town seemed quieter than he had ever known it. Along both sides of the street were doors that were padlocked, the windows looking empty and dead.

He reached the house to find the Lord family sitting down to supper. While they ate, he told them about the harvest and showed them the palms of his calloused hands.

91

"Well," said Frank, "you can rest contented. The *Spectator* came out today. It says half of the able-bodied men have left the settlements for the gold fields, with more going every day. Some women haven't been as lucky as Hattie. They have had to get along by themselves."

Boone turned to Jenny. "Have you seen Mike? Would you like to walk up Canemah Hill after supper?"

There was a moment's uncomfortable silence. Jenny blushed and did not answer. Mrs. Lord jumped up, abruptly, and began putting the dishes in the dishpan. Frank's face darkened a little.

"I might as well tell you, Boone. Mike Trahan has gone."

Boone swallowed hard, his throat tight and hurting. *Not Mike,* he thought desperately. *Not Mike, too....*

Jenny put out her hand and her warm fingers curled around Boone's arm. "We noticed for several days that there'd been no portage down from Canemah. Pa started to go up, but he was busy so I went instead. The flatboat was tied up at the float. The rigging was down. The cabin door was padlocked. We've come to know what that means. Even so, I couldn't believe that Mike had gone off to California without a word. I went down to the Indian village at the falls and found one of the oarsmen. He pointed a finger toward the south."

Mrs. Lord rattled the dishes in anger. "Mike Trahan spoke out so boldly. So sure that the gold find would make a market for Oregon. No wonder he went off like a dog with his tail between his legs. I'm not surprised that he was ashamed to say good bye."

"Moss Hartman was predicting just the other day," Frank said, "that Oregon City would become a ghost town."

Boone had not said a word. Now he looked up sturdily.

"We're not going away, are we, Frank? And soon the immigrants will be coming in."

The storekeeper laughed bitterly "The immigrants? They've come . . . all five of them. Came over the Snake River Trail while you were away."

Five—where last year there had been five hundred. Maybe it was true, maybe Oregon City *would* become a ghost town. Tears came to Boone's eyes.

But Jenny had had more time to digest the news that came to Boone all in a lump.

"Good heavens," she exclaimed, "we're not ghosts yet! Come on, Boone, I'll race you to the falls!"

VI

All that autumn and winter the fate of Oregon was in the balance. By the end of October two-thirds of the able-bodied men had left the settlements for the gold fields. Some towns were entirely deserted; others, like Salem, had five men left, and only women and children on the neighboring farms.

Although the settlers felt forlorn and isolated, the traffic was not all one way. Occasionally a traveler came north again, to his farm and family. Some had found nothing but frost and mud and plain sandy gravel in the California streams. A few came back with fortunes in their saddlebags. These did not intend to stay. They had left the hills for the winter, saying that the mountains in the land of sunshine could be cruel and bitter in the snow. But, for them, riches lay in those wild mountains and they would take their families back with them in the spring.

The boy Boone had seen at La Fayette swaggered into Lord's store one day with a thousand dollars' worth of gold dust in his bag. He wanted to buy presents for his family and was disappointed to find so little for sale.

"It's the same everywhere," he complained. "Even when you make a strike, you can't buy food in the south country. I saw a man steal some flour because he was hungry and nobody would sell it to him. I'm glad I went because my family needed money worse than they needed my work. But I'll be gladder to get back to the farm at La Fayette where I'll eat my fill."

But on many a farm that winter, Oregon settlers went hungry. A little boiled wheat they had and milk, if there was anyone to milk a cow. If sickness came to a mother left alone with her children, there was real disaster.

The gray rains had set in when young Ed Moorehead came to the Lords' kitchen door one evening. His mother had fallen out of the haymow and broken her leg. "Mister Schmidt, the Dutchman down our road, came and carried Mama into the house," the trembling, rain-drenched boy reported. "Mister Schmidt's gone for the doctor in Milwaukie, but Elizabeth said I'd better come to tell you, because you're our oldest friends."

"I'll go out right away," Mary Lord said, dismayed.

When her husband heard the news, however, he persuaded his wife to let Boone and Jenny go in her stead.

"I suppose they would be more useful," Mary said mournfully. "Growing up in Boston and living in Oregon City doesn't fit a body for ranching. I can't even ride a horse, and no wagon could get through those muddy roads."

"You've taught Jenny to be as handy as any woman in how to milk a cow," Frank said soothingly. "But it's a shame, Hattie having to climb a ladder to pitch down hay!"

"Frank," his wife answered, "we'll have to write Ollie to come home.'

"Write him where?" asked Boone. "We haven't found a soul who's seen or heard of him at the gold fields."

It came to Boone's mind, as he was putting some work clothes in a bag, that they had heard nothing of Mike Trahan, either. Would they ever, he wondered, see either one of the fortune-hunters again?

For a month Jenny and Boone and the Moorehead children struggled bravely with all the chores on the ranch.

Hattie directed her little army of workers from her bed, where she was imprisoned in a cast.

It was not all work in that isolated homestead, however. From somewhere Hattie found the strength and courage to keep up the lessons of the older children, and she read aloud to them all from the four or five books their father had left behind. At night, until the candle burned out, they all gathered around Hattie's bed as if it were a throne and listened to her lovely, musical voice read the story of Evangeline.

As Hattie read on and on in the sad tale of Evangeline's search for the man she loved, it occurred to Boone that she was picturing herself going from camp to camp in the gold fields, looking for Ollie. Where was Ollie? What was he doing? Did he, too, long for his family? Did he worry about them as he sat before a campfire in that south country?

To Boone, these evenings were like a homecoming. The rough cabin in the wilderness, the flickering candlelight, was far removed from the household of the schoolmaster of Independence who had been his father, but the happiness of shared delight, the singing words read from a book, were the same.

Sometimes he glanced at Jenny, wondering what she was thinking. Once she caught his eye and blushed.

Later, before bedtime, he went out to the barn to see if everything was safe and snug for the night. When he came back to the house, Jenny was on the doorstep staring at the late winter stars in the wide sky.

"Looks as if the worst of the rains are over," Boone remarked.

But Jenny wasn't thinking of the weather. "Evangeline was just sixteen when she started out on her search. Just our age," she murmured. "Just yours and mine."

The cast had been taken off Hattie's leg and she was hobbling about on crutches when Frank and Mary Lord appeared at the Moorehead Ranch. Their mud-spattered wagon was filled with flour, sugar, salt, a whole side of bacon from the storehouse, and a live goose, grumbling and hissing in a crate.

"We had the wagon piled high with provisions," Mary Lord explained to Hattie while Boone helped Frank unload. "As we went along the road, we saw last year's immigrants . . . some of them still living in the shelters they raised the first season of their coming. The men were gone away, the women and children looking forlorn and hungry. At each place Frank left a goose and a side of bacon. You know how Frank is. He just set the things down in such a matter-of-fact way that many were surprised to learn he did not want to be paid. They began haggling over the price."

"I bet he felt paid," Hattie said, "in their gratefulness."

Mary Lord chuckled. "He was paid in a way that made his cheeks flame. At one of the claims an old grandmother seized his hand. 'I've been more scared since my son went down in the gold fields. But I'm not now. I know we're going to get along.'"

Jenny had been out in the fields with the children. She stood in the open doorway now, her eyes shining.

"I couldn't have done without Jenny and Boone," Hattie said, with a catch in her voice. "I suppose you've come to fetch them home now. I suppose you need them, too."

Mary Lord exchanged glances with her daughter, then she shook her head.

"I won't leave while you're still on crutches," Jenny answered quietly.

"That's what I thought," her mother agreed. "It's lonesome without Jenny, but at least I've got my two legs to walk on, and taking care of a store is not like taking care of a ranch and a house full of children."

"And you've Frank," Hattie said, holding out her hand to greet Frank Lord, as he came striding into the room with Boone at his heels.

Frank looked from one of the womenfolk to the other, letting his eyes rest last on his wife's face.

"Have you told 'em, Mary?" he asked. "What do they think of the idea?" Without giving Mary Lord time to answer, he looked back at Boone. "I've made up my mind, Boone. You and I are going to the gold fields ourselves."

"Prospecting?" Boone gasped.

"No. We're taking down a pack train loaded with flour. We'll look into the chances of getting heavy freight wagons through. We've got to help get the settlers fair prices for their produce . . . not like Moss Hartman, making his fortune by buying low and selling high."

"But freight wagons!" Hattie exclaimed. "From what I've heard, that's rough country."

"Peter Burnett and a big company went down with wagons last autumn. Doctor McLaughlin said they could get through. Big freight wagons like we'd need might have to find a new way through the Siskiyou Mountains. The cañon of the Sacramento River, on the far side, is mighty rugged."

"Do you know how to get around it?" Boone asked.

"McLaughlin says it can be done. We'll look into it on our way."

"Maybe," Jenny said eagerly, "you'll run into Ollie."

"We'll try to," Frank said, "but it's a big country."

Having made up his mind, Frank was anxious to get started. It would be a long, hard, and often dangerous trip through the southern mountains and valleys. He would need more pack horses than the dozen he already owned, and he was afraid he might have trouble getting them. A great many horses had already been taken to the gold fields. Moss Hartman had been buying all he could get for his own packing business.

Frank wanted Boone at once, if Hattie could spare him. He had hated to ask and he was relieved to find Hattie so well on the mend. The rainy season was almost over and he hoped they'd get down and back in time to let Boone come out to plant Hattie's ground for next year's crop.

VII

Before the day was over, Boone was back with the Lords at Oregon City, and next morning Frank set out to look for horses. Following his orders, Boone and Mrs. Lord cut canvas covers so that each sack of flour could be wrapped separately against dirt or rain before being lashed to the packsaddle. They packed food and camping equipment that would be needed along the way. Finally Boone brought the flour over from the warehouse, and packed the canvas bags to be lashed to the packsaddles.

So, at dawn of the morning after Frank came in with the new horses, he and Boone swung into saddle. Briskly they struck out in what both of them felt to be an important undertaking.

The weather was pleasant, the sky blue and cloudless. Boone's bell pony, trained to obey his whistled signals, took the lead. The more experienced horses followed, the new ones coming after. There were forty animals under pack, each with a hundred pounds of flour carefully balanced on either side.

The days that followed were exciting, each one a new adventure, fresh as the spring that crept up from the south. Once past the little town of Salem, they entered the upper Willamette Valley, as yet unsettled. Spurred by Boone's eagerness they came to the first mountains, marking the northern border of Indian country. Both Boone and Frank rode, now, with rifles close at hand.

"Most likely they won't be needed," Frank had said to his wife that last morning, "unless we want to kill a rabbit for stew." But Boone knew that the rifles had not been brought for hunting. The Indian tribes in this part of the country did not look with friendly eyes on white men. The guns might be needed.

They crossed the mountain by a pass, fragrant with evergreens, and rode up the valley of the Umpqua River and over the Rogue Mountains. The way led through a much larger valley, empty of human beings. Then crags loomed ahead again.

Suddenly Frank pointed ahead with a cry: "Look, Boone! Look there!"

They had wound around a hill that opened a far view to the east. The first thing Boone noticed was a heavy cloud of rising dust extending to the horizon. Underneath this cloud, there crawled steadily forward something that brought back old memories.

"Wagons!" he shouted.

"A train of settlers!" Frank was red-faced with joy, "They're well past the California turn-off! They're heading for our valleys, Boone, and no mistake!"

An hour later they met the leading wagon of the big train. The foremost man left his tired ox-team and ran forward.

"What have you got there?" he sang out.

"Flour," Frank answered.

"Heaven be thanked for a miracle!" the immigrant said. "We're mighty low on food and worried about it lasting till we reached Oregon. How did you hear we were coming, friend? I thought we would have been the first through the mountain pass, held up as we were all winter at Salt Lake."

"Maybe we just hoped," Frank answered.

Boone stared back at the horses with their loaded saddlebags, and ahead at the floundering wagons strung out across the floor of the valley. Settlers for Oregon! And Frank Lord was going to feed them without ever letting them know he had other uses for the precious flour. . . .

The sacks of flour made one for each wagon. Never once did Frank mention that it had been intended for the gold fields where he might have made a handsome profit from it. He gave it as he would to a friend who was in need.

"We thank you kindly," a woman said in a choking voice.

"I thank you," Frank said, "for coming."

The train moved on, its steady business that of putting a certain number of miles behind each day. As the last wagon creaked by along the trail to Oregon, Frank looked at the empty saddle packs, and he looked at Boone.

He said: "Well, I guess we'll have to wait to see the gold fields. But we'll go on a piece and search out the wagon route Doctor McLaughlin talked about. Then we'll cut back over the regular trail. That way we'll see both routes. We'll have to drive the horses along with us else the Indians'll think we've brought 'em just for them. Too hard to get these horses to lose 'em to the Indians."

The well-worn immigrant trail guided them as far as Goose Lake. Farther south Frank and Boone had to blaze a fresh trail through the sagebrush. On the third day they came to a river.

"Pit River, Doctor McLaughlin's trappers called it," said Frank. "We'll follow it into the mountains, then we'll cut across and turn north for home."

Frank didn't talk much. He was wrapped up in new plans and heartened by the wagon company who had thought less of California gold than of Oregon's free land. He felt hopeful that an even larger train would come over the northern trail in the autumn.

They overtook the immigrant train in its hard travel across the Rogue Mountains, and, to Boone's delight, camped with it one night. Over the campfires they visited, being asked and answering endless questions.

These people had been half a year on the way from Missouri. Early snows had kept them from completing their journey last fall and they'd spent the winter in the new settlement the Mormons were building at Salt Lake.

"That Brigham Young's a wonder," they reported. "But he's a slave driver, too. Keeps the Mormons working like they were beavers. Calls the rest of us Gentiles. We could have stayed at Salt Lake, but who'd want desert land if they could get free land in Oregon? Them as were headed for California waited there, too, until the snows were gone. After what happened to the Donners, emigrants have an awful lot of respect for the snow in the Sierras."

The mention of the Donner party sent a shiver of terror through the hearts of the travelers—those from the East and Frank and Boone alike. More than a year ago, before gold had been found at his sawmill, Captain Sutter had tried to rescue a small party of immigrants caught near his home in the height of the winter. Many of the rescuers, and almost all of the travelers led by Donner, had starved or frozen to death. The disaster had taken place not far from the spot where gold was found. The impress of the tragedy was so great that a year afterward immigrants still spoke of it in whispers.

"Not for all the gold mines in California would I cross the pass where Donner died," a stout farmer said.

"There's gold in Oregon," Frank Lord answered cheerfully.

A woman, rocking her child to sleep, nodded with understanding. "The golden fields of wheat."

The immigrants asked so many questions about land

103

claims that Frank had only a little time to hear the news of the world back of the mountains. The war with Mexico was ended, the travelers said. California and all the country to the southwest was now part of the United States. From ocean to ocean the country stretched. Half the people from the East were talking about heading westward in 1849, but Captain Frémont, who had opened the trail so many followed, was in some kind of trouble. He had been court-martialed out of the Army.

Here the talk about the court-martial became so heated that Boone could not make much sense out of it. Some said that Frémont had got too big for his breeches. Others thought the government was at fault for not making its orders clear. Nobody knew how Frémont's trouble would turn out, but all agreed that it was a shame that the man who, above all others, had made the Western settlements possible should be back in Washington.

"There he sits," a boy Boone's age fretted, "answerin' questions of folks who've never seen a desert or a snow-capped mountain!"

The next morning, in the raw and blustery dawn, Frank and Boone left the slow-moving wagon train and pressed on toward home. They had made no profit; they had not seen the gold fields. Yet they rode lighthearted and contented, bearers of great news. The worst, they felt, was over. New settlers were coming to Oregon, after all.

Soon the countryside began to hint the coming of spring. The first trilliums appeared above the greening grass. Pussy willows burst through gray winter bark, and there were days when golden sunshine splashed the green-brown hills. The winds, no longer blustery, brought bird, song, and laughter.

Daily, it seemed to Boone, there was some new sign of returning life to the settlements. Hunger, hardship, and padlocked doors still served as grim reminders. But the immigrants had come, and many of them settled in Oregon City or near it. They were drawn by the friendliness of Frank Lord, who had fed them on the trail.

When Boone rode out to the Mooreheads' at plowing time, he saw three new families building cabins. The sound of hammering was like music in the air. On the older claims, however, where the men had left for the gold fields, last year's dried-up wheat was still standing. Only here and there had a ragged strip been freshly planted. More than once Boone saw a woman or a boy in tattered clothes struggling with a balky plow.

When he came to the Mooreheads', he found Jenny and Ed turning over the soil in the front yard where Hattie's flower garden had been.

"We're planting early peas," Jenny explained, while the children shouted greetings. "You can't eat zinnias!"

"Can you eat a ham?" Boone drawled, pulling a huge one out of his saddlebag. "And cinnamon rolls and potatoes?"

"You bet we can. We've been living on boiled wheat," Jenny said, as they hauled Boone's presents into the cabin.

They met Hattie halfway across the room, hobbling on her crutches.

"Boone!" she cried, searching the boy's face anxiously. "We didn't expect you back so soon. Did you . . . ?" Her voice drifted off, the question dying on her lips. If Boone had found Ollie, he would not be standing in the doorway alone.

"We didn't get to California, Hattie," Boone said gently. "So, of course, Ollie couldn't know we were looking for him."

Boone went on to tell how they had met up with immigrants, how Frank had given away all their flour, how the new settlers had come to Oregon City.

Poor Hattie! She tried to be as happy as the others over the cheerful news, but she had counted too much on the travelers' meeting up with her husband. He would come home with gold, or without it, if only he knew how he was needed!

"I thought you'd get back in time for Ollie to put in the new crop," she murmured despairingly.

"But that's what I came home for!" Boone said. "I'm going to try my hand with a plow."

"Can I help?" Ed shouted. "Spading's girls' work. Us men will plow while Jenny and Elizabeth make a garden."

The laugh that followed the nine-year-old boy's bold words gave Hattie time to hide her disappointment. She brushed the tears from her eyes and went back to her spinning wheel, while Jenny put the ham to soak in the big washtub.

VIII

One day, not long after Boone had returned from the Mooreheads', Moss Hartman came into the store. He did not look at Boone, but spoke abruptly to Frank Lord.

"Do you know how to get in touch with Mike Trahan?"

"His address is California, I guess," Frank answered dryly. "Why?"

"I want to buy his flatboat."

Frank's eyes narrowed. "What do you want of it?"

"I mean to put it into service again," said Hartman, trying to hide his shrewdness with a careless laugh.

"You? I thought you were a pack horse man. Hear you've been making quite a good thing of buying cheap in Oregon and selling for high prices in California."

Hartman laughed again. Clearly something had him in good spirits. "So I have. But that's a mighty big thing down in California. I figure there's more ways than one to get rich. Only you have to play it smart."

"I've no wish for your kind of smartness, Hartman. Just how have you applied it to Mike's flatboat?"

"We need river trade."

"Mike figured so himself. But he couldn't get enough of it to stay in business. If he left that flatboat and went to the gold fields, he had his reasons. If he didn't intend to come back, he'd have sold his boat. It strikes me that you're thinking of the Milwaukie men and the schooner they hope to build. You'd probably like to furnish their cargo, acting as the mid-

107

dleman. But they'd never let you hold them up with your high prices. You're wrong if you figure they might."

"Then there'll be other ships," Hartman said, growing angry at Frank's straight talk. "I'm not saying what I plan to do. I only asked how to get into communication with Mike Trahan. I thought you'd know where he is, seeing as you were such friends."

"I do not. Nor would he sell to the likes of you, if I did."

"No matter, then," said Hartman. "I was only trying to save myself time and trouble. I can have my own boat built."

"Golly, Frank!" Boone cried, as the man stalked out sullenly. "He'll bring all sorts of trouble to the river!"

"That he will," Frank admitted. "But he'll have difficulty finding a carpenter fit to build a trustworthy flatboat. I think he was bluffing there."

However, in the next few days it became plain that Hartman had not been bluffing at all. Piles of freshly cut lumber appeared on the riverbank above the falls, on Hartman's side of the river. Three carpenters, instead of one, went to work, and the keel of a boat began to be laid.

"I wonder if he heard something when he took his last pack train down to California. What makes him so anxious to get a boat of his own on the river?" Frank spoke worriedly. "If I could get hold of a couple of boatmen, I'd take the liberty of starting Mike's boat up again myself. Just to discourage Hartman."

Boone had had the same thought. He had even gone up to Canemah Hill where Mike's boat was tied to look things over, but he didn't dare undertake the river trip alone.

"I could take a pack train up the valley," he suggested. "I hear Hartman's sending packers out, too, and bringing in everything he can get. But he isn't sending them south with the stuff. He's storing it at the warehouse in Linnton."

"Maybe I was right," Frank said, "about his hoping to supply cargo for the ship the Milwaukie men are building. But their schooner won't be ready for months. He seems in a hurry to get ready for something."

That night Boone lay awake, watching the stars wheel across the June sky. A startling thought came to him. What was to prevent him from going to California himself? The country that had swallowed Mike—and Ollie, too—must have some enchantment about it. Prospectors were setting out from Oregon again, now that summer was coming on. He could join one of the little bands that drifted through Oregon City every week or two. Or he could even go alone and wander from camp to camp until he found Mike Trahan.

He could look for gold, shaking rocks from the riverbeds in those little pans people talked about. If he found gold and made a fortune, he could bring it home to the Lords. Frank would miss him, but he'd get along.

What would Jenny think? Boone wished she'd come on home from the Mooreheads' so he could discuss his plan with her. Talking over things with Jenny often helped him make up his own mind. Likely she'd say it was a good idea to go down and hunt for Ollie. He would do that, too, after he'd found Mike Trahan. If Mike and he panned some gold, he'd make a bracelet of it as a present to Jenny.

He fell asleep at last to dream of rivers of gold with boats floating on them, and every boat had Moss Hartman at the helm.

Next day he moved about, so silent and subdued, that Mary Lord said he must be getting sick. She threatened to feed him sulphur and molasses. Frank said maybe he'd been working the boy too hard. But neither one of them guessed that Boone was coming down with the most dangerous disease of that year of 1849: gold fever.

Boone's mind was still churning with thoughts of California when, a few days later, Frank Lord said: "Mary will run the store today, Boone. You and I are going down to Stumptown."

Boone's eyes brightened. He had not been down to Portland since the day he brought Frank word of the gold discovery.

They saddled horses and rode up the hilly trail, past Trahan's deserted boat landing. When they reached the ferry slip, the ferry was in mid-stream, crossing away from them. It looked small and frail on the swollen brown river.

Suddenly, however, Boone's eyes were drawn to a spot downstream. A sailing ship was tied up at the oak where Captain Newall's *Honolulu* had been! The ship bore the name *Catherine*.

"A trader at last!" Frank shouted. "Hartman knew she was coming up here!"

"That seems to explain it," Boone agreed. "Did you guess it, Frank? Is that why we came?"

"No. I came to see if I could get any news of Joe Meek."

Boone nodded without great interest. In the winter, the Provisional Government had sent the old mountain man across the continent to Washington to make one more try at getting Congress to declare Oregon a territory. Since the massacre of Marcus Whitman, it had seemed important for Oregon's future that this trip should be taken, so important, that Joe Meek had been willing to risk the dangerous journey. Since the old man had set out early in December, not a word had been heard of him, at least, not in Oregon City. At any other time Boone would have been anxious to talk about Joe Meek. Now the ship across the river absorbed all his interest.

It seemed an hour before the ferry got back to their side of the wide stream. Even before it nosed in against the landing slip, Frank pointed toward the newly arrived ship and called: "Who is she?"

"The *Catherine*. Just in from San Francisco." The ferryman picked up his line and jumped ashore as the craft floated in. "What I heard is that she's under charter to a bunch of miners who came home."

"Miners!" Boone shouted.

"That's what they say . . . and all with dust in their pokes."

Boone didn't take his eyes off the ship as the ferry pulled them across the water. A gangplank ran out to the bank, and, as Boone followed Frank up along Portland's muddy street, he saw that men were coming off.

Boone pulled his horse's reins and broke into a gallop. "Frank, look! One of them is Mike! He's come home!"

It was, indeed, Mike Trahan. He recognized them and let out a howl of delight. He was at the foot of the gangplank by the time Frank and Boone reached there.

"The Lord be praised!" Trahan said. "And I never expected the two of you to come and meet me!"

"Mike, how come?" Frank asked, pointing to the ship.

The big Irishman's black eyes danced with merriment. "Myself coming home on a chartered ship?" he asked. "Now, isn't that a fitting thing for a rich man?"

"How many came with you, Mike?" Boone asked.

"A good hundred, lad," Trahan said. "We haven't been in an hour, but most of them are already headed home to their wives and children. Having none ourselves, this group of us are waiting to ease the ship up the river to Milwaukie. Then we'll load her with Oregon products and send her back to the land of magic and madness."

"Did Moss Hartman know about this?" Frank asked.

"Hartman?" Trahan asked narrowly. "Sure and it's possible. He sold stuff to some of our men. Came down with a pack train, I heard. Why do you ask, Frank?"

"Well," said Frank, "it's all plain now. He's tried to corner the cargo you hope to get and make you pay dearly for it. Mike, that man will stop at nothing to put a dollar in his own pocket."

"Do you think he's made it impossible for us to get a cargo except through him?" Trahan asked.

"Time will tell. Also, Mike, he's building a flatboat of his own. Did he know you were coming home?"

"That I doubt," Trahan answered. "I moved constantly from one likely river to another with less than no luck at all. Then, at the Calaveras River, my partner and I struck gold. Some of us Oregon men had kept in touch. When we had our stakes, we chartered a ship to sail home. But I didn't see Hartman down there. I'd guess that he was ignorant of my plans."

"He was trying to learn them through me, then," Frank decided. "He thought I might know if you were coming home. So he asked how to get in touch with you, hoping I'd drop the information he wanted. I think you had better hire a horse and go on home as fast as you can. You and Boone go ahead. I'll attend to my business and come down later."

Trahan went aboard the *Catherine* to get his few belongings. Then Boone and he rode south. They took the shorter trail on the west bank and forded the river at Linnton.

Trahan had much to talk about as they jogged along. He had been joking, he admitted, about his friends and himself having grown rich in the gold fields. They had fallen far short of that, but he had found some gold and meant to use it to build up Oregon. Trahan had enough to try the river trade again. He was even hoping to build a steamship if things turned out the way he hoped they would.

"They say the trail from the East is black with wagons . . . a

112

long parade of fortune-hunters stretching from Missouri to the Rockies, lad. When they get to California, somebody's got to feed 'em. Gold-fevered men don't stop to raise a crop. California needs Oregon products, and Oregon needs California, too."

They crossed the river and Trahan pressed on at once for his cabin at Canemah. Boone put up his horse and fairly ran to the store to tell Mrs. Lord the good news. It brought the warmest smile he had ever seen to her face, yet her eyes soon clouded.

"It's wonderful, Boone," she said. "I'm glad so many are back. But I'm thinking of all the other homes where there'll be sadness."

"Like the Mooreheads." Boone kicked at the counter angrily. "I'd like to go down there and tell Ollie what I think of him!"

Mary Lord placed her hand on his arm. "Don't feel that way, Boone. Ollie's a good, kind man. It's just that he wasn't cut out for being a businessman. Not on a ranch and not, I'm afraid, in the gold fields. If he'd had any luck, I know he'd be home by now."

Hans Richter, the miller, had come back on the ship with Trahan. For the first time in many months the gristmill near the falls was readied to grind the stored wheat. The wheel started turning the very next morning.

Meanwhile, Trahan went to the Indian village to hire boatmen. The flatboat was hauled out on the bank to be inspected, painted, and rigged. Boone would go along up the river when the boat got back into service. While the repairs were going forward, however, Frank decided to send him inland with a pack train to buy the wheat still stored on the backwoods farms.

Boone carried gold dust in a heavy bag for payment, and little scales for weighing it out. "Dust in a poke," he called it just as the returned miners did and remembered a little sorrowfully how close he had come to leaving for the gold fields, himself. He was glad he had not told anyone. The thought of leaving Oregon now seemed a weakness. Maybe, though, sometime, when years and years had passed, he'd tell Jenny— when they talked over the hard winter and recalled how settlers had almost starved in the rich Oregon country!

There wasn't much wheat to buy on the ranches between Oregon City and the Moorehead place. There would be room on the packsaddles for all the wheat they had cut when Ollie first went away. Hattie would have money enough to take care of all her needs until the new crop came in.

When he had packed the wheat, however, and weighed out the gold, Hattie pushed it back across the table.

"Take the money to Frank," she said. "It will pay our store bill. Frank's waited long enough, and it's thanks to you I have it to pay."

"Ollie'll be back with gold of his own to pay the bill," Boone urged.

"Of course, Ollie will be back," Hattie said bravely. "Then we'll be on easy street."

But she was firm about the money, and Boone carried it to Frank with a heavy heart. He reported, however, that Hattie was no longer on crutches and that Jenny looked wonderful. Then he added proudly: "Their new wheat is six inches high!"

GET
4 FREE BOOKS!

You can have the best Westerns delivered to your door for less than what you'd pay in a bookstore or online. Sign up for one of our book clubs today, and we'll send you **4 FREE* BOOKS**, worth $23.96, just for trying it out...**with no obligation to buy, ever!**

Authors include classic writers such as
LOUIS L'AMOUR, MAX BRAND, ZANE GREY
and more; PLUS new authors such as
COTTON SMITH, TIM CHAMPLIN, JOHNNY D. BOGGS
and others.

As a book club member you also receive the following special benefits:
- **30% OFF all orders through our website & telecenter!**
- **Exclusive access to special discounts!**
- **Convenient home delivery and 10 days to return any books you don't want to keep.**

There is no minimum number of books to buy,
and you may cancel membership at any time.
See back to sign up!

*Please include $2.00 for shipping and handling.

YES! ☐

Sign me up for the Leisure Western Book Club
and send my FOUR FREE BOOKS! If I choose to stay
in the club, I will pay only $13.44* each month,
a savings of $10.52!

NAME: _____

ADDRESS: _____

_____

TELEPHONE: _____

E-MAIL: _____

☐ **I WANT TO PAY BY CREDIT CARD.**

☐ VISA ☐ MasterCard ☐ DISCOVER

ACCOUNT #: _____

EXPIRATION DATE: _____

SIGNATURE: _____

Send this card along with $2.00 shipping & handling to:

**Leisure Western Book Club
20 Academy Street
Norwalk, CT 06850-4032**

Or fax (must include credit card information!) to: 610.995.9274.
You can also sign up online at www.dorchesterpub.com.

*Plus $2.00 for shipping. Offer open to residents of the U.S. and Canada only.
Canadian residents please call 1.800.481.9191 for pricing information.
If under 18, a parent or guardian must sign. Terms, prices and conditions subject to change. Subscription subject
to acceptance. Dorchester Publishing reserves the right to reject any order or cancel any subscription.

JOIN NOW!

IX

The *Catherine* stood to in Milwaukie, waiting for her cargo. Word of her presence went through the settlements and with it the news that her charterers would pay the going California prices for produce. When the flatboat came back from the first trip up the river, Boone reported gleefully to Frank: "For once Hartman wasn't as smart as he thought. The upcountry settlers are very angry at the way he tried to cut them out of the profits. They had lumber and wheat and cured meat and dried beans and cheese and crocks of butter at every landing. They're determined to make up a cargo for Mike just to show Hartman where he gets off."

Frank Lord was not so cheerful. "In honest competition Mike could hold his own. But Hartman can be underhanded while Mike can't. It's that I'm afraid of."

As the goods piled up along the river, it was loaded on the ship. Settlers from miles around came to see the *Catherine* off for California.

Other Oregon men began coming home, braving the overland trails, or coming in skiffs on the river. Some came loaded with gold. Others, less fortunate, returned sick and broken by the hardships of the rough life in the camps

Whenever he saw a tired-looking rider pull up in front of the store, Boone felt a start of hope that it might be Ollie. Jenny had come home for a short time and reported that Hattie was getting discouraged and low-spirited. Other families, whose men were still at the gold fields, were getting let-

115

ters. Hattie had not heard a word. Good news or bad—anything would be less worrying than this silence. Boone found it hard to understand Ollie's behavior.

The *Catherine* had made two trips to California and the new wheat was almost ready to harvest. Boone was just home from a river trip and was helping Frank weigh up bags of salt when he saw a man come stiffly across the store porch. A heavy beard and a cap almost hid the man's face, but there was something familiar in his build and walk.

"Look, Frank . . . isn't that Ollie?" Boone whispered.

Ollie came through the door. He was thin, his shoulders stooped, and he looked dejected.

"Ollie!" Frank cried. "Welcome home!"

"Hello, Frank," Ollie said. "How are you, Boone? I stopped to pay my bill, Frank, the way I promised when I left. I've got enough gold dust to pay it." He emptied his poke on the counter doggedly. "I want it attended to."

Frank looked at his friend closely. "That cleans you out, Ollie?"

"For the time being," Ollie admitted.

Boone started to speak, to explain that there was no longer anything owing. The wheat Ollie had left had been worth more than the gold that had caused such heartache. With a gesture, however, Frank Lord silenced him.

"Why haven't you written your family?" Frank asked gently.

Ollie dropped his glance to the floor. "Well, Frank . . . how could I tell them I'd kept none of the big promises I made them? That at times I didn't even have enough to live on? From one day to the next I hoped I'd have good news to write. I'd wait for it and . . . well, it never came."

Frank reached out and began pouring the dust back in the flattened bag.

116

"You take this home to Hattie," he said. "She's already paid the store bill. Your last year's wheat did that. The wheat you walked off and left."

"Hattie saved the wheat? She did that?"

"Hattie and the children and Boone," Frank answered, thrusting the bag into Ollie's hand.

"Boone?" Ollie echoed, looking across the counter, with tears gathering in his eyes.

"Sure," Frank said. "Boone and Jenny sort of adopted your family, who fared better than some whose menfolk went away."

Ollie did not answer. His face turned red, and then pale.

"You'll be wanting to get home, man," Frank said hurriedly. "Don't you want some presents to take with you, for Hattie and the children?"

Dumbly Ollie held out the little bag of gold dust again. "You . . . you choose 'em, Frank."

Frank refused the offered payment and began pulling things from the shelves.

"You take that bag of gold home like I told you," he said. "Your credit's good at this store."

An hour later they sent Ollie out of the store with all the load his horse could carry. After he had gone, Frank looked at Boone with a warm light in his eyes. "He'll be all right, Boone, now that he doesn't have to feel ashamed before his wife and children."

Jenny came home that same day, riding the horse she had kept out at the Moorehead homestead. Her eyes were bright with happiness.

"I don't think Ollie will leave again," she reported with satisfaction. "When he saw how the wheat was growing, ready for a new harvest, there were tears in his eyes, I noticed."

"Boone's moving up to Canemah. Mike Trahan is making a river man out of him," her mother said. "So we get our daughter home and lose our son."

Frank laughed. "Only the old folks stay put. How's Hattie, Jenny?"

"She gets around well enough," Jenny reported. "Boone, are you sure you want to go to work for Mike?"

At Boone's nod, Frank said: "Almost anyone can turn storekeeper, Daughter. But it takes long training to make a good, safe river man. We'll be needing that kind of man. Before long the rivers will be the blood stream of the settlements."

In the afternoon Boone hiked up the rocky Canemah trail to Trahan's cabin. The flatboat was tied up at the bobbing landing float. Cheerful smoke lifted from his clay chimney. The Irishman had seen Boone on the trail and stood, smiling, in his doorway.

Supper was waiting. It consisted mainly of a fish Trahan had got from the Indians. Afterward, he showed Boone the Spanish comb and shawl he had brought up from California for Jenny.

"The Mexican girls wear them down in California when they fix up for a *fiesta*," Trahan said. "It's a sight for the eyes, to see them walking on the plaza with their bright clothes and combs sitting high in their dark hair."

Jenny will look just as fine, Boone thought, but she won't look any prettier dressed up than she looked in the springtime in the Mooreheads' field, helping to guide the plow.

Boone found his new job exciting. There were cargoes to be picked up at every landing. The gold dust brought into the settlements had made a great difference in trading. Store bills had been paid in all the towns. Merchants could now buy new goods, and there was a form of money with which to pay the workmen. Sawmills, carpenter shops were being started up. Everywhere the flatboat stopped—at Butteville, Champoeg, or La Fayette—Boone saw new activity.

Meanwhile, he was learning the rivers. At high water there were the strong, swollen currents to navigate. Later, there would be danger from shallows. Boone had already mastered the task of loading the boat so that it would ride evenly. Now he learned when and how to set sail, how to direct the rowers, how to steer. The thirty-mile stretch of water unrolled in his memory, every safe channel, every rock and sandbar.

On an evening in early March, Jenny came riding up the trail, hair flying, eyes shining with excitement.

"Meek not only reached Washington!" she cried. "He's already back with us! And the territorial governor is on his way from San Francisco . . . General Lane. He's going to be the first governor of the Territory of Oregon!"

"Territory?" Boone shouted.

Jenny nodded happily. "We've been a territory since before Meek set out, without knowing it, and Oregon City is to be the capital. Joe Meek's hard journey was worthwhile, though. He's been made the territorial marshal!"

All through the evening they talked about the wonderful change. Jenny said that Congress had acted to create the Territory of Oregon on August 13th—almost seven months ago.

"It's not surprising that word took so long to reach the settlements," Trahan said. "The news of the gold discovery, right at our door, took almost as long, last year."

Trahan had heard of General Joseph Lane. He was a hero of the Mexican War.

"A hero for our governor," Jenny sighed happily. "And Joe

119

Meek for marshal. He's the most famous mountain man in all the world."

"And now," Trahan said, as they rode down the steep trail to take Jenny home, "there'll be such a train of immigrants as never has been. We'll get our share, in spite of the glitter of gold to the south of us."

Suddenly Boone remembered the dream he had had the night before Trahan came home, the hard winter night when it seemed that leaving Oregon was the only thing to do.

"I dreamed once that our river was a river of gold," he said.

"A river of gold? Sure, and why not." Trahan laughed. "Yellow with wheat going from all the settlements down the stream."

X

There came an evening in the cabin at Canemah when Trahan said in a matter-of-fact way: "Tomorrow I'm going down below the falls to see to some business with Absolom Hedges. He's talking about a new mill here on Canemah Hill, as soon as convenient."

"We'll tie up?" Boone asked.

Trahan smiled at him. "That we will not. I'm thinking it's time you made a trip by yourself."

For a moment, doubt filled Boone's mind. But he saw that Trahan had none.

"I'm ready if you are," Boone said slowly.

"That's the spirit, lad," Trahan answered.

The next morning Boone started upriver in command of the flatboat. The hours went by without incident. The flatboat was above the ferry crossing when it came time to tie up for the night. Boone and the Indians cooked supper on the bank, then slept on the boat as it rode on its lines. After a campfire breakfast, they were on the river again.

They dropped off freight at Butteville and again at Champoeg. Late in the afternoon the boat was nosing up the Yamhill River toward La Fayette landing. Boone was on time and proud of himself.

The next morning he picked up an almost full load at La Fayette landing alone. At the Dayton shore side, when he had dropped downstream, he and the Indians soon had the flatboat as heavily loaded as it could safely be.

Boone planned to lay overnight at the Dayton landing. An early start the next morning would give him a daylight trip going home. He and the oarsmen made camp on the riverbank. Dusk crowded upon them, then darkness came. Shortly after, Boone grew aware of a horseman clattering toward their fire.

The rider was from La Fayette—the man who had placed the big load aboard at La Fayette landing. He called out a friendly greeting from the distance, but when he came into the firelight, there was a grim set to his face.

He said: "Boy, do you know Duke Stagg?"

Boone's brow knit in puzzlement. "Sure. He's a great bully. But Stagg's not around much any more. He packs to the gold fields for Hartman."

"Well," said the settler, "he and another man, name of Slade, sidled into La Fayette after you left. Asking about you. Stagg questioned me real close to find out if you're alone, without Mike Trahan along. I've got everything I own on your flatboat. I'd hate to see anything happen."

"You think they're up to mischief?" Boone asked. The old fear of Duke Stagg swept over him.

"There're not the kind to be up to any good. Will you make a landing anywhere going down?"

"I won't need to," Boone answered. "If anything, I'm already overloaded."

"Then the only time they could get at you would be tonight. You keep your eyes open."

"I know something better than that," Boone decided. "I'll start down tonight."

"That would be risky, too, wouldn't it?"

"Better than waiting here with those two about."

Boone was more disturbed than he had wanted to let the settler know. Stagg and Slade might have come to La Fayette on business of their own. The questions they had asked about the flatboat might have grown from idle curiosity. Boone saw a frightening possibility, however, even more clearly than had the settler who had warned him. If anything happened to damage or sink the boat, it would be charged to his inexperience. Yet Trahan would be responsible for the value of the lost freight, and would lose his boat. Hartman would like to see that happen and was capable of hiring men to try to interfere with his safe return.

The more he considered it, the surer Boone became that he ought to start down the river at once. Stagg would expect the boat to go down by light of day. If he had plans for causing trouble, he could be outwitted by an immediate start and a nonstop run to Canemah.

The Indians could understand only a little English, and Boone's knowledge of their speech was limited to a few commands. When he tried to explain what he meant to do, they shook their heads silently. They feared the night and did not want to run the river in darkness. Somehow Boone got them to understand that a greater danger threatened if they waited for daylight. Silently they hoisted sail before the moon came up and slipped quietly from the landing.

Boone had done his best to learn the twists in the channel, the islands, the shallows that lay before him. Now he had to risk everything on how well he had mastered Trahan's teaching.

He made the last rapids of the Yamhill River and swept out into the main river. After that the current carried them at a slower speed, there being a wider expanse of water. At first he was tense and uneasy, but slowly confidence rose in him and he settled down to the long journey.

Midnight found the flatboat moving past the town of Champoeg. Boone fought down a temptation to put in there and tie up for the rest of the night, on the chance that he had now left Stagg far behind. Dare he take the risk? He decided that it was safest to keep on.

The boat made a sharp bend at Fish Eddy. Not far below the bend lay Rock Island, a most dangerous stretch of water. There the hills pinched in against the river. The channel grew much narrower and was broken by three large islands and a dozen mid-channel rocks.

Then, at the end of the narrows past the first island, a sharp right turn had to be made in a matter of seconds. Below that were yet more of the treacherous rocks. In the gray light before dawn, Boone could already see the ghostly shapes of the hills creeping closer.

At last they were right on hand, on either side of the river. The first island loomed due ahead. With his steering oar, Boone swung the flatboat over, trying to recall the exact positions of the midstream rocks. The boat slipped through a channel that fingered past on the far side of the island and was caught in the rushing water of the other passage.

Boone was about to breathe a sigh of relief when a loud, ripping report burst through the sounds of the water. Before he understood what was happening, the stern steering oar was torn from his grasp and flung violently into the churning water.

He let out a cry of alarm. He had now no means of steering the heavy, lunging craft, except as the Indians could manage it with their much lighter oars. If the boat hit a log or a rock, the current would overturn it.

Boone yelled for the Indians to use their side oars, might and main. They had been dozing quietly, their services not needed. Boone's outcry brought them into action as a rock swept by on the left, missing the hull by no more than inches.

The island on their right stood apart from the lower one

opposite. Now came the sharp turn required to pass safely between. The oarsmen bent to their oars, dragging right and rowing hard across. The big lurching boat turned slowly. The island loomed, slipped over, then appeared to rush by on the left.

Immediately the boat was bearing upon the lower, midstream rock. Again Boone ripped out his orders, calm now, determined to do his best to save boat and cargo. The oarsmen pulled at his command. The craft lost speed as it came into wider, slower water, and cut in gently to the shore.

As soon as it was beached safely, the Indians started a fire and silently began cooking a breakfast of smoked salmon and tea. By the time the food was eaten, day was breaking.

Boone hated the thought of leaving the flatboat tied up here, while he made the long walk to Canemah through the woods. But there seemed nothing else to do. The steering oar had been torn away and also its housing. There was the danger from the falls. If only he hadn't tried the river run by night!

Then the Indians, all of them experienced river men, signed that they were willing to risk drifting down to Trahan's landing. So, as the light strengthened, they put out again on the water, clinging to the shore and steering with the side oars.

By mid-morning they tied up at home. Trahan was not at the cabin. Impatiently Boone struck off for Oregon City. He had gone but a little way down the trail when he saw the big Irishman striding toward him.

"Boone!" Trahan called. "Is something wrong, lad? Or have you beaten my own best time?"

"There was trouble, all right," Boone said. "The steering oar caught on a rock I didn't remember. It's my fault for trying to run the river in the night."

125

He told Trahan everything that had happened from learning of Duke Stagg's mysterious questions and the decision to try to outwit him. Moment by moment, the Irishman's face blackened. He questioned Boone closely. Then shaking his head, he said: "I don't think the oar was caught by a rock. There would be none where you were. I know that stretch well. It could have been a snag washed in by high water."

"You don't think that, either," Boone said, watching Trahan's eyes.

"Not with Stagg asking questions in La Fayette. I'm thinking they made plans for your first trip up the river without myself along. The damage could have been done by a rope stretched across the channel, just right to catch the oar. They knew I might be experienced enough to ride it out safely. They didn't expect you to do it. There's where you fooled them, lad."

Boone's heart pounded. "They could have learned that I started down in the night. Horses could have brought them to Rock Island ahead of me. They laid their trap. When the damage had been done, they took the rope up again. They expected the boat to wash into something and turn over."

"With seven men drowned, perhaps," Trahan said in a bitter voice. "You've prevented that. You're won your spurs, lad, if the saying fits a river man."

"What will you do about it, Mike?" Boone asked.

Trahan shook his head. "They laid their evil plan well. There wouldn't be a trace of evidence. The questions Stagg asked are not enough to prove anything. But we've been warned clearly of the kind of men we face. The gold fields didn't make me rich, as I told you. I couldn't stand many blows such as losing my boat and my cargo. And Hartman's craft is about ready to hit water. With my boat at the bottom of the river he would have all the new business."

"Will they try the same thing again?" Boone asked anxiously.

Trahan shook his head. "Not that or anything at all, very soon. Two accidents would certainly arouse suspicion."

The flatboat was unloaded, wagons hauling the produce on down below the falls for shipment to the gold fields. Then the boat was pulled onto the repair ways at the Canemah landing. Trahan was his own boatwright, and he set to work making repairs, Boone helping.

"We'll keep our suspicions to ourselves," Trahan said. "I have no wish to accuse another when I might be wrong."

XI

By mid-June Mike had built a second flatboat, which he handled himself, while Boone took care of the other. Moss Hartman's boat was on the river, too, and there was trade enough to keep the three craft busy.

Two schooners had come in from the East to take lumber and flour down to the gold fields. The Milwaukie schooner was launched and the *Catherine* also made regular voyages. These ships carried garden produce and eggs and cheese to help feed the flood of immigrants already pouring over the mountains.

The portage road had been improved and the new trail opened for overland trade between Oregon and California. Boone would watch the pack trains going by without envy. He was glad to be a river man. As Frank Lord had said, the rivers were the life stream of Oregon Territory.

One evening Frank came up the Canemah trail in the late summer twilight. Smiling, he said to Boone: "Jenny complains that she sees very little of you. She wants you to go out to the Mooreheads' with her on a day Mike can spare you."

"Tomorrow's as good a day as any," Trahan put in promptly. "I'm thinking, lad, you're due a little vacation."

"Why, I'm not tired," Boone protested. "Is anything wrong at the Mooreheads'?" It was still in his mind that Ollie might be drawn to hunting his fortune in the gold fields again.

He was still a little concerned as he hiked down the trail the next morning. At the store Jenny finished waiting on a customer, and then untied her apron.

"I've got a pack load ready for the Mooreheads," she said.

"Are they in trouble again?" Boone asked anxiously.

Jenny smiled. "You wait and see."

Boone brought the horses around, and they set off briskly. Boone noticed that even this back road had been improved. Boulders had been rolled to one side and chuckholes were filled.

As they neared the Moorehead claim, Boone pulled up his horse. Pointing to a rolling field above the road, he said: "Somebody's done a lot of slashing of timber. That's a freshly opened field."

"Ollie's work," Jenny murmured.

"He's clearing more land?" Boone asked. "Then he won't be going back to the gold fields?"

"Not Ollie. Papa says he brought something better than gold from California. Horse sense. And wait till you see how he's made the cabin larger and more comfortable."

They rode in to the homestead to find Ollie working at the barn. Jenny went to the cabin, but Boone stayed to water the horses at the trough and to visit with Ollie.

"I don't know how to thank you," the older man said a little shyly, "for helping Hattie with the harvest. I wish I could pay you in money."

"Pay me by raising that new crop," Boone answered.

"That I will. Had I been home where I belonged, Hattie would never have fallen out of the haymow. It's a fearful madness that can get into men, sometimes," Ollie said. "It's no wonder the Indians call the gold 'bad medicine'."

"How is Hattie?"

"Almost well again, although the doctor says she might always limp a little. Maybe that's not all bad. It will keep me reminded that I nearly lost so very much for so very little."

129

By the time he had seen the cabin, with new cupboards and furniture that Ollie had built, Boone knew why Jenny had planned this visit. Yet the improvements in the homestead were less important than the change in Ollie, and the happiness of his wife and children. Boone knew that the family was safe now, that it would prosper and grow with the country.

He and Jenny had dinner there, and started home in mid-afternoon.

"Thanks for getting me to come out," Boone said. "Seeing was twice as good as hearing about it."

By the time they rode back and put the horses in the corral, Frank Lord was locking up the store. Nothing would do but Boone must stay for supper. So it was in the moonlight that he walked up the Canemah trail to Trahan's landing. The two flatboats were tied up at the landing, and a stack of clean, yellow planks, newly sawed, above the float.

"We've got a special job to handle!" Trahan called from the cabin door. "And a big one it is. A new ship is standing at Milwaukie. Virgil Armitage came in on her, and him long gone. He's brought the machinery for our first steam sawmill. Went East from San Francisco to buy it, once he had earned the money in the gold fields. Sailed the long way round the Horn, coming home with it."

Boone blinked. There were a number of sawmills in the wooded sections of the settlements now. Some of them were operated by hand, others water-powered. But steam! Even the States had few enough of those.

"Where will Armitage build it?" he asked in excitement.

"At the mouth of the Tualatin River. That's where we come into it. We're to bring the machinery here and portage it to his mill."

"On a flatboat?" Boone gasped.

"On both of the flatboats lashed together. We'll check

130

them over. That's why I had those planks brought up. I've got carpenters to do the work. I'm thinking you and I will go to Milwaukie tomorrow and watch them unload the machinery. We'll get an idea of the size of the job."

Next day, as they came to the Milwaukie landing, Boone saw that there was a buzz of activity around the great ship. A pair of big longboats had been tied together and decked over the way Trahan's would be. They were ready to receive the machinery for the schooner. Capstans would do the heavy work of hoisting, but a dozen men—sailors and workmen, in buckskins—stood by, waiting for Virgil Armitage's orders.

At last, the big man with his fiery red beard shouted a command, and then climbed the ship's ladder to the deck. The boom swung over. Boone heard the line tighten with a creak and a groan, and slowly a huge iron boiler rose into view.

It rode in a sling, lifted by the slow turning of capstans, until the boom swung over the rail. Again came the creaking of the ropes as the giant piece of machinery settled into place on the lighter. The men fell to work with timbers, making a cradle to hold the boiler in place. Other and smaller pieces followed the boiler until it seemed the lighter could hold no more.

"How are they going to move it?" Boone asked.

"She'll be towed to shore by flatboats," Mike answered. "We'll have more of a problem when our turn comes. It will take both of our flatboats to make a deck big enough. That will leave us nothing but skiffs for towing, and we'll be in more dangerous waters."

"What if Hartman tries to bother us?"

For all that there was profit for both in the river trade, Boone knew that Moss Hartman remained a threat. The man was not satisfied to share the trade with others and especially not with Mike Trahan, who gave better prices to the farmers.

131

Besides, Hartman envied Oregon City folk because the population was growing faster than Linnton and it was, furthermore, the capital.

"I have Hartman in mind," Trahan said soberly. "If we can do this job, it will give me the money to buy a steam engine for myself. I'll build a steamboat for the river trade. Then Moss can have the flatboats to himself!"

The machinery took nearly a week being portaged from Milwaukie to Trahan's landing. Meanwhile, Trahan and Boone grew more and more uneasy about the job ahead. On the evening when the boiler stood at the landing, Armitage came to Trahan's cabin.

He said: "Mike, I've had the offer of help from no less than Moss Hartman. I think we should accept it."

"From Hartman?" Trahan asked narrowly. "And when did that man begin to offer help to anybody at all without a private reason?"

"Just the same," Armitage said, "it would take a load off my mind, as well as yours. He's offered the use of his big flatboat to tow us. It's got the sail and oar crew to do it handily. Considering the danger of the falls, I think we should accept."

"Considering the danger of Hartman himself," Trahan snapped, "I think we should turn him down. Unless he's willing to turn everything over to me. Would he be?"

"Well," said Armitage, "he's got his own boatmen and crew, you know. I realize he hates you, Mike. But with me it's different. I can't see why he wouldn't want a big sawmill next door to his town and business. I think there would be less risk in accepting his offer than in setting out on the river, right above the falls, without power enough to handle the lighter."

"I have to agree with you there," Trahan said without enthusiasm. "That's worried me for fair. And, after all, it's your machinery."

"Fine," Armitage said, openly relieved. "His boat will be in tomorrow, he says. If we're loaded, we can start on up the day after."

Trahan was thoughtful for a long time after Armitage left. Then he said: "I have no choice, Boone. And maybe it's only my pride that makes me hate to take help from a man like Hartman. We'll see that we're not caught napping."

The next day the machinery was reloaded. The masts of the flatboats had been removed. The hulls rode side by side under the temporary decking. They sank less deeply into the water than the two long boats had done. Trahan went to great pains to see that the load was well balanced and securely fastened.

That evening Hartman himself appeared at Trahan's cabin. In a tone of friendliness he said: "Well, I've given my men orders to swing over here in the morning to take you in tow."

"Thank you kindly," Trahan answered. His eyes were clouded and his mouth was grim. Boone knew he was thinking of what had happened that dark night at Rock Island when Duke Stagg had tried to sink the flatboat.

"I'm glad to help," Hartman said. "Virgil Armitage's mill will be a big thing for the towns here by the falls."

"I'm glad you see it so. A year ago," Trahan reminded him, "you were predicting ghost towns all along the river."

"I was wrong. Good night, sir. My men will report to you in the morning." With a nod, Hartman turned toward the door and left.

"Maybe he's been won over," Boone said hopefully. "Frank says Hartman has the knack of smelling a dollar a mile off."

"Just the same, lad, we'll keep an eye on that machinery until it's safe at Armitage's mill site."

Trahan sent Boone to bed, but did not lie down himself. With the light inside the cabin put out, he could see the nearby landing clearly. He was taking no chances on the lighter's lines being slipped to let it drift down to the falls.

Boone awakened at daybreak to see Trahan still seated in a chair, quietly watching out through the window. Fred and Tom, the two men who had helped portage the machinery from Milwaukie, arrived soon afterward, ready for the two on up the river. They all went down to the boat landing. Hartman's big flatboat still rode idly on its lines at the far landing.

"They'd better hurry it up," Tom said. "We've got no daylight to waste, this day. Isn't Armitage going along, Mike?"

"So he said," Trahan answered.

"Whoa . . . there they come now," Fred said, pointing across the river. "And Hartman with them."

Boone wondered where Hartman's Indian crew was. He could see only Hartman, Armitage, and three other white men.

They ran up sail and cast off. The helmsman used the river breeze to steer a course upstream, clinging close to the far shore. Then the boat quartered over and came back on the near side.

When the craft had edged into the bank above the lighter, Moss Hartman jumped ashore.

He said: "Virgil tells me you'd rather navigate the towing job yourself. So I said we'd bring the boat over and leave it with you. But I'd better leave my helmsman. He'll take your orders."

"Why, I thank you," Trahan said, and Boone noted the

134

quick relief in his face. Turning to Boone, he added: "Go muster our rowing crew."

Hartman and two of the men who had helped bring the boat across the river took their leave at once, disappearing down the portage road. Armitage and the helmsman remained.

Armitage said: "Well, I guess that proves there's some good in the worst of men. Hartman seemed to understand your wish to handle the job yourself. He was quick to suggest this arrangement."

"Whatever the reason," Trahan said, "I'm grateful, Virgil."

Boone was soon back with the dozen oarsmen needed to pull the huge flatboat. Meanwhile, Trahan had secured a heavy line to the lighter. Enough distrust remained in him that he inspected Hartman's boat quietly but carefully. He seemed satisfied with his findings, and secured the free end of the line to the towing bitt, fastened to the frame on the stern.

Once again he checked the knots on either end of the towline. Then he flung a look upstream and said: "Helmsman, we'll move first under oar. Then the sail."

"Just sing out," the man replied, furling the sail.

Boone felt easier than he had for days. The run to the mouth of the Tualatin River was not a long one, but they would have to take it very easy. Their tow was heavy and even Trahan lacked experience in that kind of work.

The Irishman gestured to Fred and Tom to cast from the landing. The oarsmen gently tightened the towline at the same time. Now, cautiously, they put their strength to the blades. Slowly the towboat began to move. All hands on the flatboat watched anxiously. At last they were fairly upon the river, going upstream.

"Easy as shooting fish in a barrel," Boone decided finally.

Trahan's patient voice coached the Indians steadily so they kept an even pull on the towline. Presently the strange craft was well out in the main stream. As the current strengthened, it was plain that the oarsmen would need the help of the big sail to maintain headway. Quickly Trahan began to cut it into the breeze. The towline stretched tighter, as they picked up speed.

Then, without warning, the flatboat seemed to leap forward. Boone was thrown to his knees. He heard Trahan yell and managed to look back in time to see the snapped towline hit the water.

Driven ahead, Hartman's boat was already twice as far away from the lighter as it had been. The clumsy craft in the rear was slipping back, toward the falls.

"Heel about!" Trahan roared to the helmsman. To the Indians he cried: "Bend your oars, lads . . . bend them now . . . !"

Boone knew what had to be done if they were to keep the lighter and its precious machinery from drifting down to the falls. Unable to help, he could only stand and watch with racing heart.

He glanced at the helmsman, Hartman's man. Had this thing been planned? Had the helmsman a hand in the accident? The man seemed as shocked as Trahan himself, or as Virgil Armitage, whose runaway machinery was racing toward the falls.

The flatboat began to gain on the lighter. Flashing oars drove the flatboat closer. Presently they were cutting in beside the runaway. By then, Trahan was standing on a boat seat, muscles straining, and Boone suddenly realized what the big man meant to do. He was going to leap aboard the drifting lighter, gather in the loose towline, and pass it back to the men on the flatboat. It would be a dangerous try but just possible if they could overtake the lighter in time.

The gap closed between the vessels. Trahan leaped, his powerful legs driving him straight out, over the water. He caught hold and pulled himself onto the lighter. Scrambling forward, he got hold of the towline and began to gather it in.

With tight throat Boone saw that they had come into the rushing water above the lip of the falls. Above the roaring waters, he heard Armitage's shout. "Mike . . . let it go! Ten times that machinery isn't worth your life!"

Had Trahan heard? If so, he paid no heed. Swinging the coiled rope above his head, he cast it at the flatboat. Boone caught it. He felt the line drag and cut at his hands. Others reached out for the rope, adding their strength to his. Tom scrambled to make the line fast to the mast.

Boone noticed even in this moment of high excitement that the tow bitt was still at the end of the line. The metal and not the rope had given way, causing the disaster.

"Get back aboard us, Mike!" Armitage yelled.

"Be off with you!" Trahan answered. "Take in the slack!"

But Armitage had his eye on the falls, looming closer. He ordered the helmsman to swing back against the lighter, and he all but pulled Trahan off.

Again the flatboat heeled about, tightening the line as it did so. But the time Armitage had sacrificed to rescue Trahan had been costly. Even with oars and sail pulling hard, the towboat seemed unable to halt the dreadful pull toward the falls.

"It'll take us over, Mike!" Armitage cried. "Cut it loose! Let the machinery go, I say!"

Trahan looked at the faces of the men in the flatboat. For an instant his eyes closed. But this time there was more than his own life in the balance, and his decision was prompt.

"Cut the line, Tom," he said. "And be it on the head of the man who planned it."

Planned? Trahan thought this horrible accident was planned? Boone stared at him, trying to read his mind.

There was no time to loosen the knots that bound the towline to the mast. Tom took a hatchet from the boat's toolbox and did the job.

Boone had never dreamed there could be moments such as those that followed. Free, the flatboat swung out of the dangerous current and made for shore. By the time it touched the bank, the lighter had come down upon the falls. There was an instant in which it seemed to hang between brown water and blue sky. Then with a rush it was gone. By the time Boone stood on dry land again, emptiness filled the spot where the lighter had been.

Now black rage stood on the face of Mike Trahan. He loosened the cut end of the towline from the mast and stared for a moment at the piece of towing bitt to which the rope was still tied. He looked at the stern of the flatboat and the other part of the bitt.

"Cunning," he breathed. "So cunning he fooled us all."

"Hartman?" snapped Armitage.

Trahan's narrowed eyes looked at him. "There is nothing I have to say, Virgil. There are only the thoughts in my mind."

"Well, that bitt was certainly a poor piece of work on the part of the smithy that made it."

"Not when it was first fashioned, I'm thinking," said Trahan.

Lunging toward Hartman's helmsman, Armitage roared: "Do you know anything about this, man?"

"I think not," Trahan answered for the fellow. "He worked hard to save the lighter."

The man looked at Trahan in relief. He said: "Thanks. All I know is that Hartman was anxious for you to use his boat.

138

And it's the Lord's own mercy we didn't all go over with the machinery."

They started down the portage road, afoot, to get in below the falls and see how the lighter had fared. Boone had no hope that anything would be left of the boats because of the rocks below. The drop and the weight of the machinery would smash and grind them to bits.

When they came in against the river below the falls, he saw a disheartening sight. A ragged shelf of rocks circled the inner horseshoe of the high falls. The boiler was hung up there, awash, but in plain sight. Nothing else was to be seen.

Armitage and Hartman's helmsman moved off without a word, toward Oregon City. Trahan and Boone returned to the flatboat above the falls.

When they came to where it was tied up, Trahan again took the faulty tow bitt in his hands, examining it closely.

"Anybody would say the bitt just snapped," he muttered. "This boat never made a heavy tow before. Hartman will be as surprised as can be that a fault developed. It's pretty he's sitting, lad."

"I don't understand it, Mike," Boone said.

"He had several days to prepare for this," Trahan explained. "I'm thinking he tempered this bitt to the point where it would snap under great strain. Yet it looked all right. There was nothing to warn us it was weak. He didn't even let his helmsman know. The man seems honest. Moreover, it was to Hartman's advantage to have the fellow as shocked as the rest of us. He surely took me in, and he's finished me."

"Won't you be able to build new flatboats?"

"Not after I've made good to Virgil Armitage. Which I must. I promised to put his machinery at his mill site. I failed in that, but I'll stand the loss myself."

Boone clenched his fists helplessly. "Hartman will have the river to himself."

"That's his hope," Trahan agreed. "It was a master stroke in the lights of a man like him."

"You'd ought to report your suspicions to Marshal Meek, Mike."

"A useless thing," Trahan said. "What proof have I? You can't accuse a man without proof."

XII

Word of the river disaster had spread far and wide. Armitage's plan to build a steam sawmill had aroused great interest. There was added shock in the fact that Mike Trahan, also, had been put out of business, all in a single stroke. No one seemed to suspect Hartman, and he played his part well. He expressed himself as horrified that his boat had failed to stand up to the towing job.

Then an unexpected thing happened. When the Linnton blacksmith heard how the accident had happened, he was white with anger.

"Why, I've been working iron and steel for twenty years," he said to a crowd in Frank Lord's shop. "East and west, you can't find a man who would accuse me of doing poor work. Except Moss Hartman! If that bitt was over-tempered, then it happened after it left my shop. Maybe it happened after Hartman got the notion of lending his boat to Mike Trahan."

Frank reported the blacksmith's words to Trahan and Boone. "It's set a lot of people to wondering," he said. "Nobody can quite credit Hartman's turning helpful without some trickery behind it."

"It still proves nothing at all, Frank," Trahan pointed out.

"Not yet, anyhow," Frank admitted. "Mike, I came to tell you that everything I've got is yours, if you need it. You've got to stay in business."

"I can ask no man to assume my debts," Trahan answered.

Frank smiled. "Then you're going to have to fight off a lot

of others who want to help you. There's no proof, as you say. But there are the characters of two men, you and Moss Hartman."

Some of the old glow came back into Trahan's eyes. But he only spoke of the chances of recovering at least some of the lost machinery. Both men were hopeful, although the undertaking would be big, slow, and costly. Neither brought out the fact that it would also be very dangerous. If the boiler could be reclaimed from the river, the smaller pieces of machinery could be made by local blacksmiths.

Moss Hartman had sent men over to bring back his flatboat that afternoon. The next morning it set sail upriver, as if it had played no part in the accident. Right after its departure, Absolom Hedges appeared at Trahan's door.

He said: "Mike, it's my feeling that Hartman's foul play will hurt him more than you."

"Who mentioned foul play to you, Absolom?" Mike asked.

"Everyone knows it was that," said Hedges. "Whether or not, I can tell you it has decided me on something I've dreamed about for a long while. You know I've been taken with your talk of putting a steamboat on the upper river. My land would be a good place to build and base it. On the other hand, a shipyard would be good for me. It would bring workers, new settlers. Pretty soon I'd have a town on my holdings."

"Ah," said Trahan, "but that takes money such as I've never had. After this trouble, I'll have none at all."

"As a result of this trouble," Hedges returned, "your friends are standing up to be counted. Friends can be more useful than money. Now, I've done well in the tannery. I hope to do better from selling town lots here, and there'll be the store and sawmill. I mean to help you build a steamboat as soon as I've got enough money."

Trahan's eyes had begun to gleam. "Meanwhile?" he asked.

"Meanwhile," said Hedges, "you'll find there are plenty of other men ready to put you back on the river."

"I'm wondering," Boone said, "how many offers of backing Hartman is getting now."

Hedges snorted and took his leave.

Withal, Trahan had one driving purpose: to deliver the sawmill machinery to the mouth of the Tualatin River. He was determined to make good that promise before giving thought to his own river trade.

In Boone there was a mixture of feelings. Happy as he was that Trahan would not be ruined, he disliked the thought of Hartman's being free to strike again. The man had acted not only against Trahan but against all the settlers.

While Trahan was occupied with trying to rescue the machinery, Boone had free time. He gave great thought to the matter nagging at his mind. He felt that it ought to be made public that Hartman had probably struck at Trahan twice before. Once, on that fearsome night at Rock Island. But he knew that Trahan would not accuse Hartman without proof and Boone could not speak out without Trahan's permission.

Duke Stagg came to Boone's mind. Stagg was the kind of man Hartman might have used to do this last piece of dirty work. Stagg might be made to talk. Boone decided that he could tell Frank enough to enlist his help. He struck out for Oregon City and waited at the store until dusk when the last customer was gone.

"You know how strict Mike is about saying things to the damage of others when he can't back it up with proof," he said to Frank. "So I'm going to tell you something I wish you wouldn't ask too many questions about. I have reason to think Duke Stagg might know something about why that towing bitt snapped."

"Stagg?" Frank said. "It could be. He's no good. He's been in and out of trouble ever since he came to this country. And he's worked mostly for Moss Hartman. What do you have in mind, Boone?"

"It might be easier to get the truth out of him than out of Hartman."

"That it would . . . if he knows anything."

"If we could prove Hartman deliberately caused that accident, then he would have to stand the damages, wouldn't he?"

"And probably go to jail as well," Frank agreed.

"Suppose somebody told Joe Meek about Stagg?" Boone said slowly.

"The marshal can't bring charges on the little you've told me," Frank answered. "However, if anybody could get anything out of Stagg, it would be Joe Meek. I'll get in touch with him and drop a hint."

A few mornings later, Trahan and Boone had finished breakfast and were washing the dishes, when an unexpected visitor appeared at the cabin door. The man came so quietly that there was no warning of his approach until his shadow fell across the floor.

"Why, Joe Meek!" Mike Trahan swung about. The marshal all but filled the doorway. He wore buckskins and moccasins and a trapper's hat, and on his jacket the badge of a U.S. marshal.

"How are you, neighbors?" he boomed.

"Now, what would be bringing you here?" Trahan said, as he motioned the visitor to the only comfortable chair.

"Legs and moccasins, friend." Meek let out a gusty laugh. "I thought I'd like to tell you myself that I've just

144

clapped Duke Stagg into jail."

"Stagg?" Trahan looked puzzled. "And what for?"

Meek winked at Boone. "Searched Stagg's cabin. Come upon a deer rifle somebody stole from Harley Pleasant three months back. Thought you'd like to know."

"Why would I, now?"

Again Meek's laugh rang out. "To be honest, friends, whether you're interested or not don't matter. I only wanted it known that I had come to see you and young Boone right after locking Stagg up."

"You want Hartman to know!" Boone exclaimed, and smiled back at the huge marshal.

"Wanted anybody who might be worried as to what's up to get the news," Meek stated. "Moss Hartman or anybody else who's had underhand dealings with my prisoner. Can't tell when a man's in jail how much he'll talk, that's all. I just thought it wouldn't hurt for me to be seen comin' up Mike Trahan's trail."

"Now, I wonder what that one's up to," Trahan muttered, when Meek had gone as suddenly as he appeared.

There was nothing for Boone to do except tell him how he had gone to Frank. "As far as Meek is concerned, he's as smart a man as ever lived. Keeping alive in the Rocky Mountains all the years he did, he couldn't help but be pretty smart."

"The more you talk, the more bewildered I'm getting." Trahan laughed. "But one thing is plain. If Duke Stagg knows about that tow bitt, then Hartman won't feel easy having him in jail."

"It's what Meek would call a b'ar trap," Boone answered cheerfully. "I sure hope Moss Hartman sticks his paw in it. Joe looked good, didn't he, with that marshal's badge on his shirt?"

It was a couple of evenings later that Frank Lord came up the trail. "Who do you think is in the jailhouse now?" he chuckled. "No less than Moss Hartman!"

"What's that?" Trahan gasped.

"Your ears aren't deceiving you," Frank reported. "Hartman has the cunning of a fox, but in Meek he met his better. Hartman tried to break Stagg out of jail last night. Meek was expecting it and waiting."

"So that's it," Trahan said, and his face broke in a smile. "Our friend Hartman wanted to send Stagg packing before he began talking."

Frank chuckled again. "It's the first time I ever heard of a man being arrested for trying to break *into* jail. But that's the charge Meek made against Hartman. Now both the black-guards are telling on each other. Stagg is trying to lay it all on Hartman, with Hartman blaming Duke. It's got them both in so deep, they'll never get out."

"Hartman and Stagg both in jail?"

"But that doesn't matter much, Mike. All Meek wants is to scare Hartman so bad he'll leave the country. If that's all right with you. He sent me to find out."

"I've no wish to fill up the jail," Trahan said. "If Hartman will make good for my boats and Armitage's machinery, and relieve us of his company, that's all I ask."

Frank nodded. "I knew you'd feel that way so I've already made some plans. The other Linnton merchants will buy Hartman's stock and the store building. I'll buy his packing business. If anything is left after he pays damages to you and Armitage, Hartman will get the money, fair and square. And I thought maybe you'd like to take over his flatboat to run, until you and Hedges get a steamboat built."

"But will the man agree to all that?" Trahan asked.

"He'll have his choice between agreeing or serving a long term in prison. I'd think he would jump at the chance to get off so easy. He's done for in this country and I think he'll realize it. Meek has called a meeting tonight at my store to settle the thing. You needn't come if you don't want to."

"And I don't," Trahan said, "not with people like you looking after my interests."

Boone stood up. "I wasn't invited to the meeting, I know, but I'd kind of like to visit with Mary and Jenny."

"And be within earshot to hear how the meeting turns out," Frank said, winking an eye at Trahan. "Jenny's already taken a perch on the back step of the store. You young ones have more curiosity than a couple of jack rabbits!"

It was dark when they came into the main street but light was pouring out of Lord's store window. As Frank let himself in, Boone could see over a dozen men inside, besides Joe Meek and Hartman. From the glimpse he got of Moss Hartman's scowling, frightened face, Boone had a feeling things were going to turn out as Trahan would wish.

He slipped around to the back and took a place, still as a shadow, beside Jenny. They were talking in low tones when suddenly the back door opened and Joe Meek appeared. His weather-beaten face looked relieved and pleased. Then he slammed the door shut.

His booming voice sounded above Boone's head in the darkness. "Business meeting in there. I reckon there's some big buyin' an' sellin' goin' on. Can you fancy it, boy? All I done was lock up a man for stealin' a gun and another for breakin' into jail. An' we get two less citizens of Oregon Territory. Two we can do without."

"Two less," Jenny said, as the old man tramped away. "But a thousand will come over the trail when the wheat is ripe . . .

147

and another thousand, and another. Every year, until the land is peopled."

Boone was silent—almost as if he was listening for the creaking of the immigrant wagons—and another sound—the sound of a steamboat whistle on the river. Then, as his thoughts drifted boldly, he wasn't just listening to a steamboat whistle on the river. He was at the ship's wheel, the ship that Mike Trahan would build.

"Do you remember when I used to be scared of the river?" he asked, a little awkwardly. "That's funny, isn't it? And me, a river man." He stood up abruptly. "When we get our ship," he said, "I'm going to ask Mike to let me name her."

"Are you?" Jenny whispered, so low Boone could hardly hear her question.

"Sure I am. I'll name her the *Jenny*."

Jenny was glad of the darkness so Boone couldn't see that she was blushing. But he probably wouldn't have noticed anyway, she told herself, as he trudged off, whistling, toward the Canemah trail.

Comanche Prairie

Giff Cheshire completed this short novel in May, 1955. It was sold on June 6, 1955 to Helen Tono at *Ranch Romances*, one of the few pulp magazines that still existed at the time. The author was paid $315.00. Helen Tono was a truly fine editor. She prepared the manuscript for publication under the author's title in *Ranch Romances* (2nd November Number = 11/18/55), but certain lines were inserted to emphasize the romantic conflict with the two ranch women, an aspect of the story quite alien to Cheshire's conception. Therefore, for its first book appearance, the text that follows is a combination of the author's original typescript and the published version.

I

Torp could feel the heat of his embarrassment change the color of his face. Rita Jordan always fussed him with her careless, headlong ways. They were downright awkward, just now, with April listening and frowning into the sun-dusted distance of the prairie.

"So that's the road herd," Rita was saying, "that you're going to take to Kansas."

"Aim to try," Torp acknowledged.

"Well, if any man can put it through, you can. Can't he, April?"

At the moment April appeared to think that if he could, anybody could, but that was because of Rita's soft-soaping. They sat their saddles, the three of them, on the edge of a big holding ground. The plains wheeled about them, wild and empty except for them and the cattle and the cowpunchers holding the loose herd.

The cow camp was off to the left, where a couple of Crown riders—from Rita's own spread—were drinking coffee and watching. They looked as if they were wondering when old Buck, her father, or Arch Campion, the man she was engaged to marry, would put a pair of hobbles on her that would hold. So far nobody ever had.

"I'm sure Torp'll do fine, Rita," April said.

They were as unlike as two girls could be—Torp Toynbee thought. Rita was tall and dark, April small and fair. April had a right to look a little stern about Rita's flirting with him,

151

Torp thought. He had shown April a great deal of attention the past year.

What made them both so uneasy about Rita's prattle was the fact that Buck had given Torp the job of trail boss, when it had seemed sure to go to Arch Campion who was Buck's ramrod as well as his future son-in-law. Rita seemed more than pleased that Torp, to his great astonishment, had been picked by Buck to make the hard drive.

Of course, there had been a face-saving excuse for Arch— he was too badly needed on the spread—but everybody knew Buck hadn't wanted to trust fifty thousand dollars' worth of cattle to Arch in the Indian and outlaw country. Arch knew that. He was a lot less pleased about Torp's getting the job than Rita seemed to be.

"Well, I just dropped by and I'd better get home," Rita observed. "You coming, Torp?"

He shook his head. "Not right now," he said, and didn't bother to explain why.

"Then *hasta luega.*"

Until later—why did she have to say that right in front of April?

"*Adiós,*" Torp said. At the moment that expressed his feelings much better than did her sentiment. Not that he didn't recognize her tremendous appeal. But she was another man's intended, and yet she kept getting Torp into hot water in more ways than one.

April was silent through several long breaths after Rita had touched spurs to her horse and sent it rushing into the distance toward Crown. Then she said: "Of course, being your boss's daughter, you should have gone with her."

"Now, look here . . . !"

The girl smiled tiredly. "I'm sorry. It's just that I'm so

darned worried, Torp. If anything does happen to this road herd, I'll lose Slash P."

"I know that," he agreed. "I'd feel a heap safer myself, if anybody but Jode Devers held your mortgage."

"He wants my ranch."

"And means to get it."

"He also holds Crown's paper, you know."

"Yeah," Torp said. "I figured that out, too. It's why Buck put me on the drive instead of Arch."

"I think Rita had something to do with that change."

"Against her own man?"

"Maybe there's a question," April murmured, "as to who her man is now."

He felt the acid heat of temper eat through him, maybe because he suspected that she was right. There wasn't anything explicit between him and April. He hadn't said much because she owned a pretty nice little ranch, and he was only a top hand on Crown. But he had done a lot in other ways. When her father died a couple of years before, he had left things in bad shape. The Slash P with all its problems had been dumped in April Parson's young lap. Torp had given her all the help he could. All the while he hadn't been unaware of her as a mighty fine girl.

So she had no right to think that he liked Rita's attitude or had done anything to encourage it. That attitude made him feel cheap, which wasn't what he expected from April. He stared at her through a long moment and saw her cheeks color. She looked away from him and kept her attention averted.

He swung his own attention to the road herd. There were three brands in it, Crown, Slash P, and Jode Dever's Rake. He knew it was as important to Crown as April's Slash P for the drive to be successful and a good beef price obtained at the railroad. Old Buck Jordan had lost heavily in a cattle speculation the year before. He had borrowed heavily from Devers, too. He was in danger now, the same as April was.

Torp had made a hand on two previous drives and knew what he faced. The dry drives, storms, and river crossings were bad enough, but there were also the Indians to be considered, and an even deadlier breed of white outlaws preying on the floods of cattle pouring out of Texas.

Like Buck and April, Torp, too, was uneasy about Jode Devers. He had never liked the man who always seemed well supplied with money to spend—or to lend, when his neighbors were running behind or going broke. Folks wondered how Devers came by his excess of wealth. Rake was big, but no bigger than Crown. Devers was competent, but there was a score of other cattlemen on Comanche Prairie as capable. The rumor was that they contributed more than they realized to Rake's prosperity. There was an old saying in the cow country that the longest loop gathered the most beef.

April looked back suddenly, fully into Torp's face. She said: "You're a very handsome man."

"What do you mean by that?"

"Don't you like a compliment?"

"Not when you had a special reason for saying that."

"All right, I did. You don't seem to realize that you're very attractive to women."

"Now, look . . . !" he said angrily.

But with the little motion of the hand that was her way of taking leave, she was gone, riding swiftly, as easy in the saddle as if she had been born with the horse.

Torp had nothing left to do with the road herd. It was ready to travel in the morning. The chuck wagon was on hand, the grub box full, its bed loaded in with the provisions they would need to carry them through the long hard weeks ahead.

He had his crew made up—two of April's Slash P cowpunchers, four Rake hands, and the rest the men he had chosen from Crown. He had a fine cavvy picked and ready to move out. Once Buck had given Torp the job, he'd allowed him a free hand. Torp was well satisfied with the outfit, except for the tough hands he had been obliged to accept from Devers. Jode claimed they were the ones he could best spare.

Torp rode over to the cow camp. Slim Standbow sat there, cross-legged and with a tin cup of very black coffee in his hand. He was an ageless man so thin the boys said he couldn't throw a shadow when he stood sideways to the sun. His companion was Jess Gardens, a young buckaroo from the Cimarron. Both were Crown men. They were men Torp knew he could count on, as long as he held their respect. From the way they looked at him, Torp wondered if he was losing it already. He knew the bunkhouse whispers about his horning out Arch Campion.

"I'm going in to headquarters for the night," Torp told them.

"Are we going to roll our tails in the morning?" Slim asked.

"Far as I know."

Gardens tipped a nod toward the herd. "Man, there's a hundred thousand dollars out there. Gives me a funny feeling to drift that much *dinero* into the wilds."

"It ain't worth a red cent here," Slim said. "So somebody's got to take it to where it is worth something."

Torp rode on, aware of the distrust in everybody about this particular drive. When a man pitted himself against vast imponderables every day of his life, he got so he had a sixth sense about such matters. He had had that same floating anxiety within himself for weeks.

Torp had entered the red cedar grove crowning the rise between the holding grounds and Buck Jordan's headquarters, when he saw the horse and rider waiting in the shadows of the trees. He knew even before he could fully detect her that it was Rita. She moved the horse forward as he came up. There was a small, confident smile on her face.

She said: "I seem to have lost my comb. I was riding back to see if I could pick it up. Did you happen to see it?"

"I didn't," he said harshly, "and you never lost one, Rita. You've got to cut this out."

"All right, I waited for you. I came to the cow camp to see you, not knowing April would beat me there. It's about Arch. . . ."

"Now, look," Torp said roughly, "I've told you before I don't want to listen to your complaints against your intended. If you don't like the man any more, why don't you break it off so everybody'll know it's broken off? This way you look like a two-timer, which is a game I don't happen to enjoy."

Coolly Rita said: "I've decided to break it off, Torp. That's why I wanted to tell you."

"Tell him, not me."

"I think he knows already."

"Then why tell me?"

"I thought maybe you'd be interested."

For the first time Torp understood fully what April had meant when she had told him he should bear in mind his appeal to women. He hadn't dreamed that Rita might have ideas in her pretty head far beyond his own reckoning. She had been engaged to Arch when Torp had signed on with Crown a year ago. For a while Rita hadn't seemed to realize he had joined the outfit. Then all at once it was different.

He was a good cowhand, a better one than Arch Campion. He was younger, had better judgment, and could muster more courage in a tight spot. He knew those things as one man automatically measures himself against another, without vanity. Too late he was seeing how much Rita appreciated those differences.

"So you *are* the reason why I got the herd to take north," he breathed.

"And when you get back, you'll probably be Crown's new ramrod."

He could only stare at her, dumbfounded. "So it was a rigged deal all the time."

"Torp, please. Dad's terribly worried. He never really liked Arch, but he put up with him because of me."

"And he picked me because of you, too?"

"He picked you because you're the man that Dad was thirty years ago."

"Thanks, but I reckon I'll earn my jobs and not have 'em handed to me on a platter."

Rita smiled easily, sure of having her way with Torp as she had gained it in so many instances from a rich and pampering father. Watching her and the rich vitality of her eyes, Torp realized how much more she offered than the top job on Crown. He couldn't help feeling the heady pull of that prospect. It very easily could start changing the whole nature of a man's thinking.

"I'll be waiting for you to get home again," she said, as if she had not heard his bitter outburst.

They rode on in silence, and he felt giddy as he considered what, very much against his will, she had opened up to him. There was no real reason why a woman shouldn't change her mind about the man she wanted to marry and plenty of men saw nothing wrong with a woman's helping her man make

157

progress. It would be mighty easy to see things Rita's way.

Their arrival at Crown together stirred no outward interest, although Torp felt guiltier than he had as yet done anything to deserve. Rita dismounted at the big house steps, tossed over the reins of her horse, and with a small smile went up to the porch. He rode on to the day corral, still deep in his thoughts.

Arch Campion was there, just unsaddling his own mount. He had seen the new arrivals, but all he did was to stare at Torp a moment. He was a tall, narrow-shouldered man, considerably older than Rita, not one who could hold the interest of a woman so restless in nature. He had a weathered face, yet it was not a strong one. His hair was a washed-out brown, gray at the temples. His clipped mustache did give him a certain look of distinction, and this along with his seniority might once have impressed Rita.

Torp washed up for the evening meal with the rest of the crew, then followed them into the cook shack. He was half through his supper when Arch came in. The ramrod tipped a nod at Torp.

"The old man wants to see you," he said quietly.

"Right now?" Torp asked, his mouth full of beefsteak.

"He said right now, and I reckon that's what he meant."

Something in Arch's voice wakened a wary feeling in Torp. Putting down his fork, he rose from his place and stepped outside. Buck Jordan stood there in the yard. One look at him told Torp he was fit to be tied. He was stoop-shouldered, white-haired, and built on the lines of a bulldog. He had a long record of experience in the cattle business, was supposed to have made and lost a couple of fortunes. The war had cleaned him out the last time, and afterward he had come out onto the great prairie.

Now his bushy-browed eyes were glaring as he stared at

orp. "You ought to know by now," he blared, "that I won't ve a man on my ranch that gives a horse abuse!"

The outburst was so completely unexpected that Torp uld only stare back, dazed. "What the hell you talking out, Buck?" he asked finally.

"That horse you rode today!" Buck roared, so loud every an in the dining room must have heard and stopped eating listen.

"What's the matter with it?"

"Nothing, except it's been scratched to the meat on the anks."

"You're crazy! I never spurred a horse that hard in my fe!"

"You rode that 'un today. Who the hell put the steel to it, you didn't?"

Torp swung and headed for the day corral, still disbe-eving. He was bewildered, an inexplicable apprehension ding him hard. Buck's rules were few, but those he made he eant to have respected. Every rider on the payroll knew hat breaking one meant. They had all seen good men—even nose Buck must have hated to lose—pack their war bags and it the pike. Yet sticking to rules was the only way rough men uld be controlled in tough work in a wild terrain.

One look at the horse he had turned into the corral showed 'orp the blood marks on its flanks. He didn't say anything, ut unconsciously he turned his head to stare at Arch Cam-ion. The ramrod was standing in the yard, watching, lis-ning, and undisturbed. He had been here at the corral at the me Torp turned the horse in. But he had left, and he would ave an alibi.

Yet it would have been no trick for one of his sympathizers slip off a spur and rake that horse's flanks real hard without eing observed. In a cooler mood, Buck might have won-

dered why this had happened just when it had. But the ol
man had never been noted for reasonableness when th
floodgates of his temper burst.

"How come you noticed it, Buck?" Torp asked.

"That makes no never-mind. You know the rules and wh
happens to the bugger that breaks 'em."

"You mean I'm fired?"

"Any reason why you should be an exception?"

Torp stood there in outraged protest, yet knew that h
dared not accuse Arch to Buck. But Buck's judgment of
man should have told him that something was fishy abov
this. Rita could have told him whether there had been bloo
on the horse when they had ridden in together, but he wasn
going to drag her into it. His helplessness only added fuel t
Torp's own temper.

"I never been accused of so miserable a thing in my life,
he said fiercely. "And I don't take kindly to the first man to d
it."

"You threatening me?"

"I'm not threatening you . . . except to say you're apt to b
sorry you got so damned rambunctious."

"Get yourself ready to drag it," Buck rapped. "I'll writ
out your check."

Torp stumped into the bunkhouse and began furiously
get his few possessions together. He swung around presentl
to see that Arch Campion had come in, with Loon Mulke
behind him. Mulkey was as simple-minded as his nicknam
suggested and was all but a slave of Arch's.

"So the old man's apt to be sorry, is he?" Arch murmured

"You must have been listening real close."

"And didn't like what I heard."

"I could have said more that you'd have liked less. Wh
raked that horse for you? That idiot?"

Campion smiled. He had known full well that Torp was bound to see through the thing in a minute. But the scheme had been successful, and that satisfied him. "Naturally you wouldn't admit it," he mocked. "Not when you were getting in so well at Crown."

"Think you'll get back in the saddle now?" Torp asked.

"Who knows?"

Arch swung and went out, Mulkey faithfully dogging him. Torp had a moment's wonder as to why Campion had brought the man in with him for that little exchange. But he was too outraged by the accusation made against him to do more than accept the check that Buck gave him. Then he saddled his private horse and rode out. He saw nothing of Rita, who probably had no inkling of what had happened. He headed for town, needing a place to stay, to think and try to get on top of this thing. . . .

II

The man who stepped into the hotel room wore a star. The first thing he said was: "Torp, you're under arrest."

That was a hard thing to take without blinking when a man had just got out of bed. Torp was still in sock feet, without a shirt, his wide brown shoulders pulled high, hard, and tight.

"You're crazy," the sheriff said harshly, "if you figured you could kill Buck Jordan and get away with it in the county I was elected to law. He was as good a friend as I ever had."

"Buck?" Torp said in a hollow voice. "I don't get it, Lot. Something happened to him?"

"A slug through the back of the head, that's all. Don't insult my intelligence, Torp. You rowed with Buck yesterday. He fired you off the ranch. You made talk, before witnesses, about him being sorry. Arch Campion and Loony Mulkey brought the word to me. They both heard you tell Buck he'd be sorry."

"Sure," Torp said in a low, dazed voice. "I never mistreated a horse in my life, and I'm getting tired of having to say so. When Buck jumped me about that cayuse, then fired me without even taking time to think, I blew my own cork."

Lot Bush was a tall, thin man with a shock of wiry gray hair. He said: "Everybody on Crown knows Buck'd fire a man for pinking a horse. When he tied the can to you, you had it coming. There was no need for threats."

"I didn't mean it as a threat," Torp said desperately, "only as a warning that something underhanded was going on. I

162

was plumb floored when I saw that horse. I can't say how it happened, except it was done after I had turned the horse into the corral and gone to eat my supper. That's all I know for sure."

"Done by whom?"

Again Torp was confronted by the hard fact that he could not mention Arch's name without dragging Rita into it and cause a scandal. Weakly he said: "I won't say who I think it was, Lot, but you can figure it out. Buck would have guessed, if he'd kept his head. With him getting killed, it looks like there's more to it than even I thought. You've got to believe me. The whole thing's a frame-up."

"Wish I had a dollar," Bush said sourly, "for every time I've heard that. That killing was a dirty business. There was Buck, rocking and reading in the lamplight, the way he did before he hit the hay. You knew that was his habit . . . which made it dead easy for you to sneak up on the house and send a slug into him through the window."

"The killer was somebody who knew Buck's habits," Torp agreed, "but not me."

"Get your duds on."

The hotel room, already hot with the mounting day's heat, seemed to whirl about Torp. He could only keep on standing there staring at the old lawman, bewildered, lost, and sickeningly afraid. Then despair drained into him, and he obeyed, not fully conscious of the motions he went through getting on his boots, then his shirt. He started from habit to strap on his shell belt, but Bush stepped over and took possession.

It was like a bad dream to Torp, when he tramped down the creaky stairs of the hotel and went out through the lobby, the officer following. From the stares he got from the desk man and a couple of cowpunchers in the lobby, he knew that

163

he had been among the last to hear the news of Buck's murder.

In a nightmarish kind of stupor, Torp went to the ramshackle courthouse and let himself be booked into jail. Finally, seated on the bunk of a cell, he stared out, for the first time in his life, through bars. He watched Bush turn the key on him, then go out through a farther door that closed off the last of his liberty. He was too numbed even to think for a while, but then the memories came flooding back. He had been promoted to trail boss. He could remember Crown's ramrod who was almost Rita's husband. Then he thought of his real wants—to succeed with the drive, then ask April how she felt about him. Afterward, full awareness of what had happened came to him and with it the full pain.

All the while he had been planning and hoping, deep and dark things had been going on, undercurrents hidden from him, the schemes of men in which he had been chosen to play a part which he could not have dreamed. Had there been anything to warn him, he might have taken steps to protect himself. But there had been nothing—except Rita's obsessive interest in him.

But there was more to it than that. The vaster, deadlier thing had to do with the mortgages on Crown and Slash P held by Jode Devers. Arch Campion had perhaps seen the handwriting on the wall, had known he was losing his hold on Crown. Devers, in anything he might be planning to do, would have found a crafty foe in Buck. But Buck was out of the way now. There was only Rita left, without experience or competence in the actual management of the ranch.

The day grew hot and seemed to have no end. He was the sole occupant of the jail, which was a cramped, smelly adobe structure behind the courthouse. Restlessness kept him pacing the hard-packed earth of the floor, and he smoked cigarette after cigarette in his furious thinking. He was no longer mystified as to what maneuvering had put him here. The urgent, frightening question was what he could do to save himself and protect April's interests in what he now felt would come.

It was some time in late afternoon when he heard a sound at the outside door. Then the door cracked open, letting in a flood of the day's hot light. Torp shoved up from his bunk, staring. He could see Bush outside, but the sheriff did not come in. Instead, a smaller figure stepped through into the outer space of the jail and crossed at once to the bars that made a separating wall. By then, Torp was standing there, his eyes narrowed dangerously as he looked at Rita Jordan.

She turned, glanced back at Bush, who closed the door reluctantly. Then she fixed her gaze on Torp. Her face showed strain, perhaps anguish, and he knew what a shock to her Buck's death had been. They had been close, she the indulged darling of a rich old man, given her way so much that she had come to expect anything she wanted. She was different now. With her new, subdued manner she was even lovelier than before. No man with any feelings would ever deny her physical appeal. She was slim and supple, and her dark hair and sun-browned features gave her a look of vitality that was rich and promising. As she watched Torp for a silent moment, she didn't seem as aroused against him as she would have been if she believed he had killed her father. He grasped the bars with his hands as he looked at her.

Softly she said: "Don't glare at me, Torp. I know you didn't do it."

"Then you're a freak," he blazed. "Everybody else thinks otherwise."

She nodded. "I know that. Especially out at the ranch. But

it was made to look like you did the killing, and it was just too pat. There's too much about it that doesn't fit you at all . . . at least for anybody who knows you and keeps cool enough to think straight."

"Thanks."

"I couldn't accept it when it happened. I can't yet. I know you never abused that horse. I know you couldn't shoot a man in the back. That's why I came to see you. I'm afraid, Torp . . . terribly afraid."

"That makes two of us," he answered.

"It was the only fair thing to do," she said in a rushing way, "but, when I told Arch I meant to break it off, I sealed my father's doom."

"So you think that, too, do you?" he murmured.

"I'm sure of it. Torp, he means to take Crown away from me since he can't get his hands on it any other way. It would be easy. If I can't meet the mortgage payment to Jode Devers, Arch will get the ranch."

"You think they've thrown in together?"

"I'm sure of it. Arch has known how things were going. He's made dark hints that maybe I'm not as smart as I think. He's turned the crew against me. They think it was my bitching around that got Dad killed. They won't take my orders, I know. I'm completely helpless."

Torp heard that with an inner groan. "They've teamed up," he agreed. "That makes plenty of sense. I already figured Devers might want to take over that herd on its way north. Arch could be a big help to him. They've stuck a bargain. What's being done about the road herd?"

"Arch has taken over the trail boss job again. I told him he was fired, and he just laughed at me. He said they were trailing right after Dad's funeral tomorrow."

"Oh, Lord," Torp groaned.

"You've got to stop it, Torp. You're the only one who can."

"From here?" he said with a snort.

"You can get out." She turned her back. He saw her tug out the tails of her blouse, then tuck them in again. When she turned back, she held a hacksaw blade that she handed to him. "And that's how. I sneaked it out of the smithy shop before I left Crown."

He swallowed. "My God, Rita . . . jumping jail . . . !"

"Torp, if you'll do it, I'll pay any price you ask."

He stared at her, aware that she was not qualifying that promise. A day ago she had been only an inconstant girl changing men. Now she saw everything slipping away from her—the father who had provided so well, so indulgently, already gone, the means of her future privileges about to go.

But that did not decide him. He was thinking also of April when finally he nodded. "I'll do it. And you better get out of here before Lot gets to wondering if you aren't already sawing me out."

"Where'll I see you?"

"You won't," he said.

"Torp . . . you won't leave the country?"

"Of course not. But Bush is going to know where I got this blade, even if he can't prove it. I don't reckon it'd be good for us to see each other, even on the sly."

She nodded a reluctant acceptance of that, and then was gone.

The only place he could hide the hacksaw blade was in the top of his boot. The mere possession of it made him feel jumpy. But he didn't think it would take very long to saw through one or two of the bars on the small, high window in the outside wall of the cell.

Around six o'clock the old courthouse flunky brought him

his evening meal. He saw no more of Lot Bush. After the flunky had gone, Torp decided to do the cutting while the town was still noisy. He fell to work at once.

The bars set in the adobe had been tempered but could not resist the sharp saw blade. He had the first one out quicker than he had expected, and set to sawing the second. It proved a little tougher, and his fingers were sore by the time he got through. In another five minutes he was outside, pressed against the back wall of the jail, his heart seeming to run wild in his chest.

For the first time he gave thought to the problem of getting out of town. Rita might have helped him there in advance, but he had felt that she had risked too much, already. He also lacked a weapon with which to defend himself, a fugitive in a country strongly aroused against him. His first act in that status had to be to steal the first horse he saw that could be taken with any kind of ease.

Prowling his way across the first side street, he entered the darkness of the farther alley. This brought him deeper into the heart of the town, increasing with it his dread of being discovered. A moment afterward he could see up the slot between the buildings a brightness of street lights. Two men crossed that narrow brilliance while Torp watched. Turning into the slot, he began to move carefully toward the main street sidewalk.

Just short of the walk he halted, his eyes yearningly on a horse that stood in hip-shot stoicism at the tie bar he now could see close on his right. It was a gray gelding and looked fresh. Then in a near panic of haste he pressed himself tightly to the rough, battened boards of a wall.

A cowpuncher strode between him and the horse, came even, then passed on. His jaw firming, Torp moved out then onto the walk, taking his long chance. The man who had just passed thumped on into the distance. There was nobody close at that moment.

Loosening the reins of the horse, Torp noted that it wore the brand of Dever's Rake. He climbed into the saddle and turned the horse slowly toward the closer edge of town. It was all he could do to keep from urging the gelding to a headlong rush, but he held it to a quiet walk until the darkness of the prairie had swallowed them. Cutting widely around the town, then, he struck a straight course for April's Slash P.

The road herd, tallying over three thousand head, was being held on Crown's east range. It was an hour short of midnight when Torp rode past the cow camp's low fire, not going close enough to attract attention. It was a bitter dose that a day ago he had been in charge and now was a fugitive from justice, but he accepted the change, putting what might have been behind him, setting himself to meet what now must come.

He went on, riding steadily northward. An hour later he topped a rise that, in the starlight, let him see a huddle of headquarters structures that was small compared to the big Crown and Rake outfits between which April's ranch lay. The buildings sat in a hollow on the great open plain, straddling Sage Hen Creek and its long, lush belt of cottonwoods.

Torp had never known Hank Parsons, April's father, who had established the spread back in the days when the Comanche Indians had been a fierce hazard for the cattlemen. But he liked what he had learned of Hank from April and the three cowpunchers who had stood by her so faithfully. He didn't know yet, but he doubted that any of them would believe that he had actually murdered Buck Jordan. He felt certain they would give him all the help they could in meeting the immediate problem.

He hallooed the house as he rode in. By the time he entered the ranch yard, there was a light in the bunkhouse. The door stood open, and the figure of an elderly man was framed in a background of yellow lamplight. It was Cal Jepson, April's ramrod. Torp knew her other two riders were still with the beef herd.

"What in blue blazes are you doing here?" Cal gasped when he recognized the new arrival.

"I busted jail. If you don't want any part of me, Cal, say so, and I'll keep riding."

"Light down," Cal said at once.

"April here?"

"Sawing wood, I reckon . . . if she's able to sleep with all her worries."

"I bring more, and I reckon we got to get her out of bed. You get some duds on and come over."

Torp swung to the ground, trailed the reins of the horse, and tramped over to the small ranch house at the edge of the brawling creek. He rapped loudly on the door, using the same knock the boys did so as not to alarm her if they had to awaken her in the night. When she opened the door to him, she gave the same disbelieving stare that Cal had. "Why, Torp," she breathed, "we heard you were in dreadful trouble. I was going to town in the morning to see you."

He was glad to hear that, to know that she meant to stand by him even when she must suspect strongly that Rita was seriously involved in the trouble. Stepping on in at April's motion, he looked at her appreciatively. In the white nightgown and wrapper, her fairness seemed even more pronounced. Her skin, with its weathering, seemed as burnished as her hair. The eyes that now regarded him in sharp curiosity were, he began to realize, just a little withdrawn from him. That was natural, a part of the price he had to pay for this ghastly mess.

170

"I'm a fugitive," he told her flatly. "I sawed my way out of jail. You're taking a chance on letting me come here, and I wanted you to know it."

"Who helped you get out of jail?"

He knew he couldn't lie to her, that it would be the worst thing he could do. "Rita Jordan"

"I sort of had a hunch."

In spite of everything, Rita had driven a wedge of steel between them. He knew that as he saw the deep hurt in April's eyes. But she didn't want him to see it. Somehow she managed to clear that lost, unhappy look from her eyes.

He told her briefly of the evidence that had been piled up against him so suddenly, so completely without warning, since they had separated two evenings ago at the road herd. Then Cal came in, grave and concerned. He had forgotten to comb his white hair, which stood up in a sleep-rumpled thatch.

"Arch told Rita," Torp concluded, "that he's starting the herd up the trail right after Buck's funeral in the morning. So we've got to act fast . . . tonight."

"Doing what?" Cal said.

"Arch has no right to move that herd when Rita's against it, not even with Devers's backing. She commissioned me to do anything I have to do to protect her interests. If you'll go along with me, April, that gives us the right to take over that herd and hold it ourselves."

"When?" Cal's eyes were showing a gleam of rising hope.

"Tonight."

"I can't let you do that," April said. "Not against Crown and Rake, both. You might take it, but you'd never hold it and stay alive . . . or out of jail."

"Let the man talk," Cal told her sternly.

"The two men you assigned to the road herd," Torp told

171

them, "used to stand their night guard together. I had 'em on the last guard of the night. That likely hasn't been changed. Cal and me will be there to contact 'em when they come on. We'll run the herd onto your south pasture, April, then cut out Devers's stuff as fast as we can and shove it back."

Cal nodded vigorously. "Holding nothing but Slash P and Crown steers. That'd put us a hundred percent in the right."

"Sure," Torp agreed. "Then if Campion and Devers persist in making trouble, you can call on Lot Bush for protection from outright rustlers."

"It's the caper," Cal agreed. "We'll do it."

Torp knew April didn't much like the idea of his acting already as Rita's new ramrod, but she seemed to realize it was the only thing that could be done, and she gave her reluctant consent.

It was around two o'clock in the morning when Torp, now armed, rode out with Cal Jepson, heading south. There was more star shine than he would have liked, although that might help as much as it would hinder them. The prairie was wholly silent except for the murmurings of the wildness and of the night. Sound beat up by the hoofs of the horses seemed too loud and carrying to Torp.

They passed the cow camp, which now showed nothing but the shadowy shape of the chuck wagon and the huddle of night horses that was beyond. They rode at a slow, stealthy gait, dreading some betraying accident. The men occupying the camp at the moment, if the Slash P riders had come on guard, would be loyal to Crown and Rake in any undertaking. They would burst into lethal action if they caught on to what was under way.

Old Cal took a long, thoughtful look at the starlit sky, then said: "Well, by now Jack and Curly should've come on. Let's try our luck." They began to cut in closer to the big herd, held

172

loosely and now bedded for the night.

They approached on the blind side of the big cattle concentration without having caused any alarm. They sat their horses then, waiting for the night herders to come around to this side on their regular circle. Soon a horseman appeared ahead.

Jack Peck came up, rendered curious and uneasy by the tone of the old man's voice. Cal only motioned to him to wait silently. Soon Curly Davies rode in from the opposite direction. Then Cal explained it, what had taken place and what they figured was yet to happen. Both the cowpunchers were deeply impressed.

"Rustling's their aim, sure as you're a foot high," Curly said. "Arch Campion brought out his toughest turkeys to replace the men you picked, Torp. They and that bunch of Devers's men make a bad pack of curly wolves. Just from the way they acted, Jack and I got scared there was something up we weren't being let in on."

"If you'd trailed," Torp agreed, "you and Jack would probably have died some night in your sougans with a bullet in your brains. If you help us in this caper, you might die of the same cause but with your boots on your feet."

"I don't mind getting killed," Peck rejoined, "as long as I get some say in how it happens."

"So let's start making targets," Curly joined in.

They discussed the procedure briefly. Afterward, Peck took the point, Cal and Curly the flanks, while Torp swung into place behind the herd. Quietly, carefully, they got the cattle lifted to their feet, gently urging as they moved their horses in close. When the steers were started, Torp was still fairly confident that the camp, so far, had not been alarmed. Still loosely spread, the herd was soon lined out, moving west the way Peck pointed it.

Soon they were putting the camp's faint shapes well behind. Yet tension only grew in Torp. A moving herd made a racket nothing on earth could silence. A trained cowpuncher slept attuned to such disturbances. It was the habit of years, which could arouse him out of the deepest sleep. Somebody was bound to wake up and realize, however belatedly, that something was going on. The men in that camp would have plenty of grounds for a lot of murderous gunfire. Then Torp could no longer see the rearward glow of light from the camp. He still heard nothing but the scuffing of the moving cattle, an occasional soft word from one of the riders.

Soon he figured they were at least a mile away from the camp, with six or eight more miles to go. He kept watching the starlit prairie behind him. Some warning intuition alerted him finally before he caught any actual sound of disturbance. Abruptly he swung his horse about, halting it and staring hard, his ears keened in intent listening.

He could see nothing in that direction except the dark black prairie, a star-fired sky above. For a moment he could hear nothing above the continuing noise of the herd. So strong was his feeling that trouble had developed, he began to ride rearward. In some five minutes he saw them, two riders coming cautiously from the cow camp.

There was only one thing to do then—try to turn them back and give Cal and his men every chance to get the cattle on to home range. When Torp had narrowed the gap between himself and the oncoming riders, he lifted his pistol out of the holster. He fired two shots, well above their heads, that served both as a warning to them and to Cal. To his disappointment, the oncomers only lifted the speed of their horses to a lope and drove forward.

Again Torp shot, and that time they swung sharply to their right. Yet they still pressed on, toward the retreating cattle.

174

They hoped to get past him, for they were convinced that they had been hit by cattle thieves. Nothing, Torp knew, could rile a rustler more than to have another rustle from him. If they failed to stop the men taking the herd, they would try to stampede it, scattering the herd.

Driving in his spurs, Torp sent his horse running at the two riders. They were returning his fire by then. At any moment the shooting would bring more help from the cow camp, where Torp knew there would be three or four more men. He drove his horse so furiously at them, disdaining their gunfire, that finally they swung their mounts fully about and drew back to a safer distance.

When they halted again, turning about to stare in his direction, he stopped his own mount. Then they went on, receding into the far night. He knew he had only gained a little more time for himself and his saddlemates. The pursuers would be back in force before very long.

When Torp started back in the other direction, he could see that the cowpunchers with the herd had lifted it to a run and were now bending it due north toward Slash P range. Cal fell back, and, when he had come together with Torp, he said: "Well, the boys can handle the stuff from here on in. You and me had better stay here to see what happens."

"We'd better," Torp agreed.

They waited there for nearly an hour, but there was nothing further to disturb the night. That puzzled Torp at first, then he began to understand it.

He said: "They don't know how many of us there are and are scared of running into a gun trap in the dark. They're waiting for daylight. Which will be coming soon, I reckon. But there's one way to gain us some more time, and I'm going to take it."

"What's that?"

"Go back to the camp and tell 'em who took the herd an[d] why. Then they'll have to get in touch with Campion o[r] Devers to find out what to do about it. Either Campion o[r] Devers would want to see the other and have a powwow. B[y] the time they got it figured out, we might have Rake's stu[ff] cut out."

Cal nodded. "They couldn't hit the rest of the her[d] without being clean off base. Just the same, son, I don't allo[w] they'll give up the caper."

"Me, neither. But we can use all the time we can buy."

"I better go to that camp with you."

"No, you help the boys. Soon as you get the herd on Slas[h] P, start cutting out Rake."

Torp rode back toward the cow camp he had himself e[s]-tablished so short a while ago. His immediate problem was t[o] gain enough time to cut out the thousand head of Rake be[ef] steers in the herd and haze them back onto Crown grass. H[e] knew that neither Campion or Devers cared enough for Buc[k] Jordan to want to go to his funeral, but they might deem [it] wise strategy to attend. Thus he might gain the greater part [of] the day for the cutting work.

III

Light was beginning to thin out the darkness as he approached the cow camp. Uneasy men watched him. They all knew and would recognize him, Torp realized. They had been isolated, but, if they had seen Campion yesterday, they would know how he stood with the law. He had a tight ache between his shoulders as he rode up to them.

Grimly he said: "You men take it easy. By now that herd's crossed onto Slash P by authority of the owners of two-thirds of it. Leave us alone, and you'll get the Rake steers back. I'm warning you. Don't give us trouble."

The men he had picked for the road crew were all gone now, he observed. Left were half a dozen hard-eyed individuals who probably knew more about the general situation than he did himself. But what he had said made them shift uncertain glances at each other.

"How'd you get out of the hoosegow?" one of them asked.

"Never mind that. Just you see you don't put Campion or Devers there by acting foolish."

It took all the nerve Torp could muster to swing his horse and turn his back to them as he rode off. But he had to do it, to deepen their uncertainty by acting completely positive about what he was going to do. Even so, he was wholly alert till he had put a couple of miles behind him.

He caught up with the herd just north of the boundary line. Cal suggested taking the herd in deeper, so they rode on closer to Slash P headquarters before they milled it to a stop.

They began the cutting work at once. There being only four men, they made slow progress. Everyone watched the surrounding country with anxious eyes.

"Well, I think it worked," Torp finally told Cal.

They were finished with the job in mid-afternoon. Then they threw the Rake steers back across the line onto Crown pasture. Torp felt enormously relieved, for now there were no technical grounds for trouble to be made over what had been done. But they had done little to mitigate the tough going that still lay ahead.

Cal figured it wise to stay and help Curly and Jack guard what was left of the herd. Torp rode on in to headquarters alone. April's relief at seeing him was clearly apparent. He knew she had worried more about her men, and maybe about him, than about her beef steers.

She insisted on his eating the meal she had cooked and kept warm, and said she would take food out to the men waiting with the cattle.

"What are you going to do now, Torp?" she asked as she served him.

"Go see Lot Bush and tell him what we did."

"*You* will? He'll lock you up again."

"Mebbe. But I don't figure to spend my life running, April. So I'd rather face the music first than last."

"Torp, you're a fine man, and I wish Lot realized it."

He glanced up at her, his breath coming fast. He wished deeply in that moment that he could tell her how much he cared, how little Rita and her offers really meant to him. But now he had no right to speak, and he might never have again. He could only look away from her, pick up his fork, and start eating. Yet he knew from her long silence that she had sensed the moment and gained from it only a disappointment.

He had barely started his meal when the sound of swiftly

178

running horses reached them. April stepped hastily to the doorway and stared out.

"Torp!" she said after a moment. "Hide! It's Arch Campion and Jode Devers!"

"There's nothing to hide from," he said grimly, shoving to his feet. "And I don't reckon they'll try to take me prisoner for the sheriff." He caught up the rifle that stood by the kitchen door and handed it to her. "Just in case. When I go in to town, I figure to do it under my own steam."

April kept the weapon and remained in the kitchen, while Torp stepped outdoors. The two riders whirled in, bringing a wash of dust with them. Their lack of surprise at seeing him here informed Torp that they had been in touch with their men at the cow camp. They kept their saddles, staring down at Torp.

The whole body of Jode Devers was restless, some pushing energy never leaving him, never fully spent. He was stocky, swarthy of complexion, and wore a spade beard. He had a nose that had been broken and badly mended and it distorted the shape of his heavy face. His eyes were prying, always busy, never warm.

With a long, brittle stare at Torp, Devers said: "Heard you'd sawed your way out of jail, Toynbee. But what was the meaning of that caper you and the Slash P boys just pulled? Who the hell give you orders to cut my stuff outta that road herd?"

"Rita Jordan and April Parsons. But let's just say we cut their stuff outta your bunch, Devers. We figured it was simpler to move the herd away from your tough hands before we did it. Now, if your curiosity's satisfied, you two can get the hell outta here."

Both the men knew that April was just indoors with a weapon in her hands. They didn't look at the doorway, and they bristled without mustering the courage to do any more than that.

"So Rita and April are going to drive their cattle by themselves, are they?" Devers asked.

"Don't see where that's any of your business, man. But if they do, you two had better lay off. We've made that herd a pretty hot commodity for you to handle, and that wasn't any accident."

It put a funny feeling in Torp to see the hate in Arch's eyes. The man had not been able to run his bluff on Rita and force her to turn the affairs of Crown over to him. He had heard from Torp himself who had gained that authority in his stead. Now he had no alternative but to work with Devers in a subordinate capacity. He blamed Torp for that.

With words hurled like stones, Devers said: "When a man on the dodge takes over a herd, he can only have one intention . . . to pick it up for himself. And the whole damned Slash P is in on it, aiding and abetting a known fugitive from justice . . . a known killer."

"April wants to rustle her own steers?" Torp asked.

"You're all out to see what you can take off of Crown."

"Rita has no say in the matter?"

"Rita Jordan," Devers snorted, "don't know one end of a steer from the other. You got her snowed under, but we don't aim to set by and watch you fleece her outta everything Buck Jordan built up."

Torp grinned at that, but his uneasiness was increasing. Swinging his horse, Devers rode out, and Campion followed stiffly. April came out of the house, still holding onto the rifle, her face bitterly determined.

"Did you get the drift of that?" Torp asked.

She nodded. "The man's found a dandy way to turn the tables on Slash P. We're harboring a known criminal and

180

working with him. Technically, I suppose, that does make us crooks."

"And targets," Torp said grimly, "for anybody's gun."

"But they must have sent word to Bush where you are."

Torp shook his head. "Not them. It's much better for me to be running loose and leading Slash P in a big rustling caper. April, if I don't hustle in and give myself up, they're going to hit you and the boys with all they've got. Mebbe they'll make off with the herd from here, instead of waiting till it's on the trail. All they'd need to claim is that I must have had some owlhoot confederates."

She nodded reluctantly. "I guess you've got to do it, Torp. But it seems so unfair."

"Lot Bush is a stubborn cuss," Torp reflected, "but I think he's fair. I'll take my chances with him."

He wouldn't have felt he had a right to do it, but when April came forward and rose on her toes to kiss his mouth, he couldn't help himself. His arms closed around her, and then their kiss, their embrace were all he had ever dreamed they would be. He couldn't ask her the big question till he had come clear of this thing, but her smile, as she stepped away, told him the question was already asked, the answer given. Then she turned and ran into the house.

He saddled a fresh horse. Although he was dog tired, he rose to leather and rode out at once for town. It was a hot, bright evening, and he rode fast and hard. He reached the town at dusk and went at once to the sheriff's office. He was lucky enough to find Bush still there. The officer looked up absently from his desk, then his eyes widened and his head reared back.

"You," he said in a wholly impersonal voice.

Torp made a cool, uncertain grin. "I figured by this time you'd be riding my sign, Lot. It should have been easy."

"Nothing's easy," Bush said with a sigh. "I had to be here this morning for the inquest on Buck Jordan. Rita told enough facts and offered enough fancies that the verdict complicated matters."

"What was the verdict?"

"That Buck came to his death at the hands of person or persons unknown."

"Then I'm free?" Torp gasped.

"Not of suspicion," Bush rapped. "But I'd have had to charge you or turn you loose. Now, I ain't charging anybody till I get to the bottom of the cussed thing."

Remembering how hard it had been for him to come in, Torp was elated as he moved on into the office and shut the door behind him. "There's one thing more I'd like to know, Lot," he said softly. "You don't think I'm guilty any longer, do you?"

"Well, I got no business saying so, but I don't. Your showing up again voluntarily about settled my last doubt."

"And now," Torp pressed, "you've got new suspicions about who's guilty?"

"It ain't my business to discuss matters like that with you," the sheriff snapped. Then he grinned slightly. "But I have. What Rita told at the inquest makes more sense than the wild yarn Arch Campion and Loon Mulkey told me the morning I flew off the handle and locked you up. I never had any doubt that Jode Devers is an out-and-out cattle thief. There's nothing I'd like better than to send him up for it."

"He's teamed with Campion, and either Campion or Mulkey killed Buck."

"Mebbyso. But that ain't proved."

"Let's start proving it."

The sheriff came forward in his chair. "How?"

"Devers wants Slash P. To get it he's got to bust April so

182

she can't make her mortgage payment. To do that, he's got to make off with her market cut. And he's going to try."

"Granted."

"Arch Campion wants Crown. Since he can't get it by marrying Rita, it's got to come through Devers's foreclosing on it. And that's their deal."

"Again not proved."

"If you caught 'em trying to move cattle they got no claim to whatsoever, it'd be proved, wouldn't it?"

"It sure would," Bush agreed.

Growing excited with the headway he was making, Torp explained why he broke jail, how they had prevented Campion's trailing out with the herd that morning, and were now holding Rita's and April's steers on Slash P.

"Then Devers shows up with Campion," he concluded, "and makes a big noise about us being crooks. That's the excuse they're going to use to put their train back on the track, Lot. Mebbe they'll try tonight."

"So?"

"You get you some deputies and make your way to Slash P without being seen. Let Campion and Devers latch onto that herd and move it far enough to prove they're stealing it. Then you take the herd back. The Slash P boys and I will pitch in any way we can."

"We'll do it," Bush said. He looked eased and energized. "But you ought to have more than verbal authority to hold onto those steers."

"If I went to Crown to see Rita, I'd be lynched."

"It wouldn't be necessary. She was afraid to stay out there. She's here in town at the hotel. You go see her, then hit for Slash P. I'll be out as soon as I can get set."

"Fine," Torp agreed.

He moved swiftly along the street. The town was quiet

183

now, darkness closing in, although the day had held more excitement in the coroner's inquest over Buck Jordan than in his funeral. Torp went straight to the Cattlemen's Cottage. To his relief, he found the lobby empty. Turning the register around, he saw that Rita was occupying room 227. He climbed the stairs and knocked on that door.

It opened at once, and Rita stood there, not surprised. "I saw you ride into town from my window," she said. "I hoped you'd come up."

He stepped on in and shut the door. Turning, he stared at her intently. He knew she was stirred by this visit and felt that events had brought them closer together than ever before. Then he told her what had happened since he had seen her in the jail and how Bush figured he ought to have her written authority for holding the Crown beef cut.

"You can have anything you want from me," Rita said softly. "And when it's settled, I want you to hire a new crew and run Crown for me permanently."

"Write me a kind of power of attorney, Rita. I don't have much time." He nodded toward the table, where there was a bottle of ink and a pen.

Turning, she went to the suitcase that stood open on a chair, and rummaged out a sheet of letter paper. He watched her seat herself, then begin to write. Neither, until that moment, had been aware of sounds in the hallway. Now, hearing, they turned. Even as they both stared at the door, it burst open. The man who stood framed there was Arch Campion. Torp could hear the rushing crash of blood in his ears.

"Seen you heading for town, Toynbee," Campion said, "and figured it might be a good idea to follow. What's going on here? What's he rooking outta you now, Rita? What's that you're writing?" He came on in, shut the door, then started toward her.

"It's none of your business, Arch," Rita said harshly. "And you get out of here."

Arch made a grab for the paper she had just signed, but Torp's hand dropped on his shoulder and spun him around. Campion's eyes went more dangerous. His fist drove out at Torp, who had seen it coming but had been unable to brace himself against it. The blow caught Torp hard in the belly, driving him back as Campion swung again. Torp dodged that one.

Not wanting a fight just then, he rapped: "Cut it out, Arch. Damn you . . . not here!"

But Arch Campion would have it no other way. He came on belligerently, belting out with his fists, making contact, driving blow after blow, first to Torp's head and then his midsection.

In self-defense, Torp had to drive back, knowing that Arch wanted to make a scandal of this thing in Rita's hotel room, that anything that detracted from her reputation was a help to him. Torp's feet scraped the floor as he bored in. He struck hard and fast, right and left, smashing Campion back against the wall. The racket that made seemed to jar the whole building.

Somewhere a voice bawled: "What the hell's going on?"

Torp heard Rita moan. He drove Campion hard against the door. The man struck with a foot, driving Torp back against the bed. Then they crashed together, both driving punches in hating rage. Torp forgot everything then but the fight. Again he crowded the man backward by the force of his driving fists. Campion slashed an elbow at Torp's eyes. He tried to kick Torp in the groin.

Then the door burst open, and men poured into the room.

"Stop them!" Rita cried.

Somebody grabbed Torp's arms, while others seized and

held Campion, both men struggling still but powerless now. Rita, her cheeks flaming with either embarrassment or anger, swung toward the table. She picked up the paper she had written out. Looking at Arch Campion, she smiled bitterly.

"You might as well know what this is. It gives Torp Toynbee authority to run Crown for me indefinitely."

The black fury in Campion's face only deepened. The men who had come stared at Rita in surprise. What a juicy thing this'll be when it gets around, Torp thought in despair. But he had to have that authority. He accepted the paper from Rita, folded and put it into his pocket. He found his hat, picked it up, and walked through the doorway.

As he thumped down the stairs, he realized that the situation had been changed considerably. Rushing to the courthouse, he found it locked. Bush was already getting set for the night's effort. Torp found him at the livery barn. He drew the man aside.

"Rotten luck, Lot," he said in a low voice. "Campion trailed me into town. He knows I went to see you. Since you let me free, he must figure you've changed your mind since hearing what you did at the inquest. That means they'll wait to see how the land lays before they'll risk jumping that herd."

"You're right," Bush said. "And it looks like Arch trailed you a mite farther than the courthouse."

"We had a little tussle, which you'll hear all about. You can't hide out on Slash P from now till they're ready to open the ball. What're we going to do about it?"

"You get your authority from Rita?"

"It's in my pocket."

"Then we're set, and, if they hold off a night or so about making their try, that's all to the good. You scout the country and see if you can figure out how Devers will work it. Then we'll know how to set our trap. Have somebody watch Devers. When they start something, you send somebody in to me hell a-hiking."

"I'll do that," Torp agreed.

He got his horse and headed out of town. The elation he had felt for so short a time—when he had learned he was no longer a fugitive from the law—was gone. In its place was a deep anxiety. *It's Rita,* he thought. *Every time I meet her, something goes wrong. There's something wrong with her. She's not crooked or indecent. There's just something she lacks.*

It was good to have his head cleared of the pull she had had on him a while. April's arms and April's kiss had made that change in him permanent. But April would not like his fighting in Rita's hotel room.

He rode in to Slash P headquarters a little after midnight. He had passed the undisturbed road herd at a distance, not wanting to cause its guards even temporary concern by riding in on it at this time of night. There was no light at headquarters. Knowing there were enough men with the cattle to sound an alarm in case of trouble, he put up his horse, went to the bunkhouse, and started to undress, meaning to appropriate somebody's bed.

He had just started to jack off a boot when Cal spoke in the darkness. "That you, Torp? What the hell . . . couldn't you find Bush?"

"I found him and was left to run loose a while, Cal. On top of that, we made some medicine for the rest of this ruckus."

"You sure make time."

Torp grinned and, sitting on the edge of a bunk, explained matters to Cal.

"I have news for you," Cal said. "Jess Gardens seen me this evening, on the quiet. He's the one real friend I ever had on Crown. He says Arch has got the crew whipped up to where it believes we all were in on a plot to murder Buck, then take over Crown through his daughter or any other way we can. They're about ready to grab you and me and the other two boys and swing us. Buck was a tough old warthog, but his riders all liked him."

"No fooling?" Torp breathed.

"Wish I was, but I ain't."

"I've got to go over to Crown, Cal, and try to talk sense into 'em."

"Think you could?"

"They're all riled and orey-eyed, but at least some of 'em are straight-shooters. I'll get over there the first thing in the morning, before they've scattered."

Torp slept the few remaining hours of the night. When he opened his eyes, Cal was getting dressed in the pale dawn light. Torp had only skinned off his boots and, groggy from piled-up fatigue, he pulled them on again. Cal, seeing him well for the first time, gave a hard stare.

"Arch got in a few licks," he said.

Torp rubbed his sore face. There was a small cut at the corner of his eye, a bruise on his jaw. Going out to the water trough, he washed himself. Then he started for the corral to get a horse.

"You better wait for breakfast!" Cal called.

"I'll have it on Crown, or else furnish a breakfast for them."

"You be careful. It's sure a death trap for you right now."

"What part of this country isn't, right now?"

Torp rode out toward the divide between Slash P and Crown. As he came down the western slant, from which he could see the big headquarters at the bottom, he saw that the day's activity there had begun. But the day horses were still in the corral, waiting to be saddled. The crew had not yet dispersed.

He could see the cogency of the argument Campion had used to hold the support of the ranch hands. Buck had been killed in a way to outrage any man with a dislike for cowardice and treachery. A clever man could easily build up an enormous blind prejudice and turn it to his own advantage. There couldn't be many on Crown besides Arch who knew what the real plot was. But misguided men could do as much damage as crooked ones.

As he entered the ranch yard, men saw him and grew alert, wary. Their hard faces told Torp that they were hostile toward him to the last man. He felt as if he had a lump of beeswax in his stomach, and he could feel a muscle tic in his temple. Yet outwardly he showed no uneasiness, as he swung a glance from man to man.

Out in the yard, from the bunkhouses and even the cook shack, they began to edge toward him. He kept his saddle seat.

"Howdy, boys," he said in a matter-of-fact way. "Where's Arch this morning?"

"He ain't around," said Joe Brownless. "Dunno what you're doin' here, Toynbee, but you sure ain't welcome."

"Look," Torp retorted, "I know you boys are on the prod and why. You think I shot old Buck in the back. I didn't. You've been sold on the idea Slash P is backing me in some kind of caper you've got to prevent. You're dead wrong. You've got to listen to the other side of it."

"What other side?"

"Campion and Devers are the ones you ought to go after, not me and Slash P."

Brownless spit out some tobacco juice. "Don't try to throw dust in our eyes. You're playing for a big pot, and we don't aim to set on our hands and watch you rake it in." His eyes and the eyes of the other men said they would string him up right now if they could take him.

The fear in Torp ran deep. He knew that the least excuse could turn these men into a dangerous mob. They weren't going to listen to reason. He studied them steadily as they kept inching toward him. His hand was not far from the grips of his gun. Yet their approach was so apparent it disturbed his horse, which began to twist nervously.

"Stand back!" Torp warned.

They recognized the deadliness of his tone. The movement stopped.

"I know you boys only figure you're righting a wrong," he said fiercely. "You just don't realize the situation isn't what it seems. There's a big rustling deal afoot. I'm not pulling it. I'm only trying to stop it. Don't let yourselves be made fools of."

"Which is what you're trying to do," Brownless snapped. "It's plain you figure to step into Arch's boots and crawl into the bed he hoped for. That's why you shot Buck in the back, and why you been making time with his one and only heir. You needed help, so you got that hard-up Slash P to back you."

"What I want to know is whether you're working for the owner of this outfit," Torp rasped, "or the man who hopes to own it . . . Arch Campion."

"Buck Jordan hired us. We figure we're still working for his interests. Arch suited him as a ramrod, didn't he? Was Buck alive, Arch still would suit him. To our minds, he still is the boss here, till Rita comes to her senses."

Somebody made a grab for his bridle, then. But even as his hand touched leather, Torp's gun was up and leveled at him.

"Let go," Torp breathed. "Now, every damned one of you

190

move back! I'm riding outta here, and, if there's a back-shooter among you, that makes twice I've pegged you boys wrong."

He waited until they had all edged over against the side of the bunkhouse. Then he whipped his horse about and sent it forward at a rush. He could all but feel their hostile attention on his back. But if anybody had the urge to knock him out of the saddle, he was ashamed to do it before his saddlemates. A back-shooting had started all this trouble.

IV

When he got back to Slash P, Torp went immediately to April's house. Swinging down at the steps, he went up, but, as he crossed the porch, she came to the open doorway. He saw from her eyes that Cal had already told her why his face was marked.

"So you had a fight," she said, "with Arch Campion."

"All right, I did. I had to see Rita. Bush wanted me to get a real authority from her to handle the cattle we're holding here. So I went to her hotel room. Arch busted in and started mixing it. Some men barreled in and broke it up. I knew it was going to look bad and how you'd feel."

"I don't suppose it's any of my business," she answered.

"A better way to say that is it's not important enough for you to think twice about it."

Her face and her eyes were hard in their withdrawal from him. "Don't you want some breakfast?" she asked.

"That's what I hoped for."

"Come on in."

She had served him with flapjacks, bacon, and coffee before she spoke again. Then she said: "Cal told me what you arranged with Bush. I think you're guessing the thing wrong."

"You do? Why?"

She took a seat across the table from him. "You could watch that road herd so hard you'd put the really big prize right in their laps. I worried all night over what Jess Gardens told Cal about the Crown boys being so hostile toward all of us. Did you do any good over there?"

"I sure didn't. They'll be on top of us any time Arch gives the word."

"That will come anytime, and probably tonight. Arch will bring Crown against us while Devers and the Rake hands do the big rustling."

"What I already figured."

"But what you don't seem to see is that Devers doesn't have to take that herd. With a nice diversion here, and all of us pinned down . . . even Lot Bush and a handful of deputies . . . Devers will be at liberty to sweep the range. Mine and Rita's."

Torp watched her with an open mouth for an instant. "I think you're right," he said finally. "You'd both go as busted if you lost a big bunch of stockers as if you'd lost the market cut. I bet you Devers has already been working at it, getting the stuff bunched up and set, while we've been so preoccupied with the road herd."

"That's my feeling."

"April, likely you're keeping a knot-headed man from playing the fool."

"Again," she murmured.

"All right, if you must believe that Rita Jordan means something to me. Even if she did, that kiss you gave me would have wiped it out right then."

"So you remember that I kissed you."

"I'll never forget. But right now we've got to do some quick planning, and get word to Bush. I'll go see Cal."

"He went out to the herd."

Torp swung back into the saddle, astonished and pleased that April had seen through the tangle of things and had discerned Devers's real plot. Torp was so sure she was right that he was ready to base his plans and make his play on her hunch.

The herd was still being grazed loosely on the south range. Cal, Jack, and Curly were guarding it closely, still as certain as Torp had been an hour ago that it was the main prize of war. He swung down at the campfire they had going under the old roundup coffee pot.

He poured himself a cup of coffee and rolled a cigarette. Jack and Curly were studying the signs of recent combat on his face, but something in Torp's manner discouraged banter.

His smoke lighted, Torp said: "No man ought to try to get along without a woman."

"I ain't trying," Curly said. "It just happens no woman'll have me."

"Devers and Campion like it fine for us to sit up night and day with this herd."

"What's that got to do with women?" Curly asked.

"April just pointed out that those sons-of-bitches are only going to make a feint at this concentration, at the most. Meanwhile they will, if they haven't already, make a big cut on our range stuff and Crown's. That's just as profitable and just as sure a way of busting both ranches."

Cal shoved to his feet, his face darkening. "By God, you're right," he breathed. "Did April come up with what to do about it?"

"That's our department. What we do, mainly, is outfox him. Arch has got the Crown boys heated up to where they'll make a pass at this ranch with pleasure. And there's the trap Lot Bush wants to set. We've got to let Crown hit us. It's the only way we can get Devers to pin the deadwood on himself for the sheriff."

"Sounds unhealthy," Cal reflected, "but smart."

194

"You have April get word to Bush, and order her to stay in town till the ruckus is over," Torp continued. "Tell Bush to get out here early tonight with enough men to handle it. Meanwhile, I'm going to scout some country I've been thinking about, then spy on Rake till Devers makes his move. Once I'm sure the ball is rolling, I'll get in touch with Bush. He better not stay on Slash P, because that might scare Crown off. Tell him to be at that old east line camp of Crown's. I'll meet him there."

"What makes you so sure it'll be tonight?" Curly asked.

"The way the Crown boys were seething this morning, they'll take things into their own hands if they don't get fighting orders from Campion."

"That's my feeling, too," Cal agreed. "We'll go on it."

Torp flipped his cigarette into the fire, put down the tin coffee cup, and went to his horse. He grinned down from the saddle, then rode out, heading northeast.

The day's bright heat and light were mounting fast. Ever since his talk with April, he had been remembering a piece of country, lying north of Devers's Rake that could lend itself easily to rustling activity. It was a patch of water head breaks, vaulting crowns of eroded badlands giving down in all directions and beginning to show courses of drainage water in its lower declivities.

It was poor range, but well enough grassed and watered that considerable cuts of cattle could be held hidden in its creases for short periods. Perhaps Devers had already started collecting Crown and Slash P range stock, taking it stealthily at night. If so, and sign could be found, it would be deadly easy to set a trap. If nothing had yet been done, it would be harder, riskier, with success depending on shrewd guesswork.

Presently, through the thick haze of the heat, he could see the low, purpled lifts of the *malpais*. His course was taking

him between there and Rake's back boundary line, which la[y]
in against the roughs. There was more than an even chanc[e]
that Devers was having this region watched, just in case. B[ut]
Torp hoped to pick up signs of cattle moving in number[s]
from the direction of Crown and Slash P.

He found none. Even when he had come to the on[e]
opening into the *malpais* through which cattle might b[e]
driven in haste, he still had seen nothing to excite him. As h[e]
remembered the country on eastward, this was the last brea[k]
in the rough rim rock that bordered the breaks.

Returning, he rode closer into the rim. Even then, it wa[s]
not until he reached April's upper corner that he found any[-]
thing. Then he came upon the tracks of a horse and fres[h]
droppings. He knew that none of April's riders would hav[e]
been there so recently. The tracks came out of a mere notc[h]
in the wall and returned. Somebody had come out of th[e]
malpais, made an inspection, then cut back into cover. Torp'[s]
breathing was speeding up.

He followed the sign in through the notch. The benc[h]
proved much narrower than he had believed, and he soo[n]
came into a small, rocky cirque. This, he discovered, brok[e]
on into a wider cañon. Then, at the end of ten minutes[']
riding, he came upon water and grass. For a time this puzzle[d]
him, since it would take forever to file a herd of any siz[e]
through that narrow stricture. Devers would have to act mas[-]
sively if he was going to take advantage of the turmoil he an[d]
Campion had created. Then a compelling hunch came t[o]
him. That man had only taken a look at April's steer-dotte[d]
range.

When the gather was made, it would come from Crow[n]
and Slash P both. There was another, better way into thi[s]
place, and that was the broad rim break he had first sus[-]
pected. There was also a good way out, through the deepe[r]

196

malpais. The cattle would be thrown in here, then passed on through the moment it was safe.

That left only the time when it would be undertaken, and Torp was still convinced the coming night would see that action. This was the place for Lot Bush to set his trap.

Dangerous though it was, he felt obliged to check his theory about the main entrance to this hidden holding ground. Again he followed the broad cañon that led south. Horse tracks showed him that the place had been visited in the not too distant past. Presently he came out onto the prairie exactly as he had expected.

He was doubly careful as he started on his way back to Slash P. Anyone seeing him in this vicinity would know that he was at least guessing shrewdly, even if he had not discovered anything. He drew no easy breath until he had got down onto more habitual range. Thereafter, he lifted his horse to a gallop and soon had come in on the cow camp.

Jack and Curly were the only ones there. Cal, they told him, had gone in to headquarters to send April after Sheriff Bush. There was little more Torp could do until the officer arrived, with, he hoped, plenty of help.

"Cal said he aimed to set up a watch on the divide between us and Crown," Curly Davies reported, "to get a mite of warning when they head our way."

"Good idea," Torp agreed.

He went on at top speed, hoping to catch April before she had left for town. He had sent instructions for the sheriff to rendezvous with him at the old Crown east line camp. Now that he had a much more definite picture of the thing they had to buck, he wanted to amend that suggestion. But when he reached headquarters, he found the place deserted. April had gone, and old Cal presumably had taken up his vigil against Crown on the divide.

It was by then mid-afternoon, with five or six hours left before nightfall. Entering the house, Torp ate a cold meal in the kitchen. Knowing that the night would demand the utmost of him, he decided that the best thing he could do was to make up some of his lost sleep. He stretched out on the old sofa in the living room and at once dropped off.

He awakened with a start as he discerned the darkness that had crept into the room. Yet the fact that nothing had disturbed him was reassuring. He realized that April had had time to get back. Although he had asked her to stay in town afterward, he hadn't really believed that she would do it. Now that the chips would soon be down, he would have liked confirming word from Lot Bush. Yet it would make it easier she was out of harm's way until this dispute was settled.

He saddled a horse and rode out to the divide, where he found Cal still on watch. Swinging down beside the old ramrod, Torp spoke in a low voice.

"I'll spell you while you go in and get a bait of grub. Better take some of those cold biscuits out to the boys. Then I'll make a beeline for the Crown line camp and wait for Bush."

"Torp, I'm worried about April. I told her to stay in town but she said she'd be damned if she would leave us to fight her battle. She should be back by now."

An instant apprehension shot through Torp. "Likely Bush made her wait to come out with him," he said.

"If she ever got to see Bush. Ever since she failed to show back, I've been seeing boogey men. Them buzzards might have been watching to see that nobody got away from the ranch."

All Torp could do for an instant was groan. If April had been intercepted, there was no telling what she might be undergoing by now. At the least, it meant that he and the three

Slash P riders would have to deal with both Crown and Rake alone.

"Maybe we're just too keyed up," he offered.

"I sure hope so," Cal said.

The ramrod rode in to get some food and take more to the men with the herd. As soon as he came back, Torp rode north again, this time heading for the rendezvous point. Suddenly every bit of confidence had gone out of him. Not only did his enemies have the initiative, but they possessed an overwhelming superiority in numbers.

By the time he reached the old Crown line camp, the stars were out. Dismounting there, he took up his lonely vigil, sick with dread, all too aware that Bush should have got here by now. He waited an hour, all he felt he dared. Then he remounted and rode out, heading east.

Bush's failure to make contact had convinced him completely that the big effort would be made that night. He had to put his worry for April out of his mind and concentrate on meeting the aggression. He was sure that Crown would attack Slash P to tie up its crew while the real rustling effort was being made. The one advantage was that the defenders were seeing further into the play than Devers and Campion expected.

His hunch was strong that the badlands portal he had visited that day played a part in the rustlers' plans for a quick getaway with the gathered steers. Once the herd was in the breaks, pursuit would be difficult, a contest for possession close to impossible. He meant to station himself at that point and wait for the action.

The night air was warm, the countryside ironically peaceful, the stars a milky brightness overhead. The wild smells in his nostrils blended with the unruly energies now pumping through his body. All he could hear was the *scuff-*

scuff of his horse's hoofs across the cured prairie grass.

As he neared the breakaway that led into the badlands, h
began to study it. He picked the left-hand side as affordin
him the best position and cut toward it. Reaching the talus
he dismounted, secured his horse to a bunch of mesquite
then climbed the detritus a distance on foot. When he ha
gained sufficient elevation to satisfy him, he halted. Fishin
out the makings, he twirled a cigarette and lighted it. Then h
settled himself to what would be a long, wearing wait that i
the end might prove fruitless.

His light, nervous sleep at Slash P had failed to restore hin
completely, and the enforced inactivity began to stupefy him
Rising occasionally, he walked about, constantly watchin
the prairie outward from the rim along which the cattle woul
probably come. When finally he grew stiff with attention, h
guessed the night was some three hours old.

It was the stirring of his horse, below him in the conceal
ment of the rock, that alerted him. He cast a searching look t
the west again, closely probing the open prairie at the base o
the rim rock. When he could make out nothing there, h
looked the other way.

Out of the deep night and well away, riders came on to
ward him. Energy pumped up in Torp, wiping away the las
trace of his tiredness. A grim satisfaction came to him be
cause of the sharpness of his guesswork. The men wer
coming from the direction of Rake. No ordinary business
could bring them to this place at this time of night.

They seemed to sense nothing of his presence as they rod
past his vantage point, well out from him and going easily
steadily toward Slash P's back range. At that distance h
could recognize none of them, but they were five in number.
It was going to be a hard thing to handle.

He saw them vanish into the west. For the moment he wa

uncertain as to the next step. It would not be well for him, he decided, to return to the line camp just yet in hope of finding the sheriff there at last. It would take a while for Rake to round up a cattle cut and start back this way. It would be better not to have too many riders moving on the prairie until he was certain that a stolen herd had been moved into the badlands.

He waited there, unable to keep his mind off April, wondering what had become of her and what by now might be happening at Slash P. When he judged that enough time had elapsed for Rake to be showing back with cattle, he descended the rocky slant and went up into the saddle. Yet he stayed in his place of concealment, trusting the horse's senses better than his own to warn him of the approach of its kind. He had not been there very long when the animal pricked up its ears, then turned its head to the westward.

A little later he heard the rumble of massed cattle. Then he could see them coming on, sufficiently spread that he knew Devers had cut deeply into April's range stock. There would be another such gather to make from Crown. That would keep Rake tied up the rest of the night.

Torp watched the herd pass him, then enter the rim break to vanish. The dust of the passing reached his nostrils, and twice he could easily have shot a rider out of the saddle. Their careless, easy progress informed him that they did not suspect spying.

As soon as he had the prairie to himself, he swung his horse and sent it streaking along the foot of the rim, knowing the herd noises would muffle that of his own travel. He rode into the line camp rendezvous to find it still deserted.

As he sat leather, pondering his next move, his heart was a chilled lump in his chest. But there was no time to think about that now, to second-guess how they might have

planned it better. Whipping his horse about, he started fo
Slash P headquarters.

He was on the last stretch when the sound of distant gun
fire reached him. His pleading had been no more effectiv
than he had judged at the time. Crown had brought its figh
to its small neighbor. For one of the few times in his life, h
used his spurs on his horse.

The mount had lost its freshness, yet it managed to pic
up speed. The steers sifting into the *malpais* were gone from
Torp's mind now, and all he thought of was his three friend
against an unknown number of foes. The sounds of th
shooting increased. It was already a stiff, hot fight.

He pulled down in the cottonwoods up the creek from
headquarters. He could see the star-lighted shapes of th
buildings, the flashing tongue darts of gunfire. Leaving hi
horse, he ran on, his gun was in his hand. The buildings wer
encircled, he realized. He could tell by the shooting from th
house that Cal's vigilance on the divide had paid off. Ther
had been time enough to warn Jack and Curly. Since none o
them believed that the road herd was any longer the prize
they had forted up. Crown wasn't having an easy thing of it

V

Standing in the trees, Torp picked his first target. He knew as he shot that he was warning Crown of an enemy at its rear, which would bring all the retaliation he could handle. Also, in shooting from this position, he would make himself a target for Slash P. Yet without hesitation he fired.

He heard a man make an outcry. Another rapped: "What the hell? Who's gettin' careless back there?"

Torp kept shooting, cutting back and forth in the trees, and in a moment was drawing fire. The men in the house divined the situation, and their own shooting grew more brisk. Yells passed back and forth in what had become defensive positions, questions without answers. There came two more sharp, hurt cries. Torp knew from the diminished shooting on this side that the men caught in the crossfire were scuttling around to the other side of the house.

Inside the house somebody was watching closely, reasoning with sharp insight. Cal's tight voice called: "Torp . . . Bush . . . whoever it is! We're coming out!"

"Come on!" Torp yelled.

The door cracked open, and men came through. Torp covered both ends of the building to make sure the ramrod and his men made it to the cover of the near outbuildings. Then he moved in to join them.

"You?" Cal breathed, as he came up to Torp. "Man, you made enough noise to be a posse."

"Your calling Bush's name is what spooked 'em," Torp

said. "Come on, let's wind it up."

They edged out, four of them now acting as a single, determined unit, and began to angle their shooting in on the far side of the house. It was returned promptly, signaling that Crown had not pulled off. Since he had seen no horses as he came in, Torp judged they had left theirs farther away. He and Cal moved down one end of the house, while Curly and Jack followed suit on the other.

Shots were returned angrily for a moment, then somebody yelled: "Come on, boys . . . let's get the hell outta here!"

"They figured they was in the right, and we're all alive," Cal said. "Let 'em go."

Suddenly there was no more shooting. In a moment the sound of half a dozen rushing horses filled in the void.

There was no time to hash it over. Fiercely Torp said: "We hit it right on the nose. Rake took a big cut of Slash P into the *malpais*. Right now they're likely making the same kind of gather on Crown. Jack, you hit for town and don't spare your horse. Get Bush out here with as many special deputies as he can scare up in town."

"I shouldn't've tipped off the fact that we expect Bush," Cal reflected. "That's liable to queer the whole thing."

"If Arch had led that attack, he'd have given the orders. I never heard him. Did any of you? Then he's probably showing Devers where to sweep on Crown. Nobody who heard you mention Bush would know about that."

"Just the same . . . ," Cal began.

"You bet," Torp anticipated. "We have to make sure nothing jumps the track. You and Curly and me are going up to that rim break and hide where I did. We'll let 'em move more cattle in, but we won't let 'em move anything out."

"Then let's go," Cal agreed.

Jack headed for town at once. Minutes afterward, the

other three men were riding to the northeast. An hour's hard driving brought them close enough to see the rough, low rises of the *malpais* in the night. Again Torp's mind was busy trying to outguess his adversaries.

The fact that Campion had kept out of the attack on Slash P was not encouraging. If he was helping Devers with the rustling on Crown, the thing probably had moved fast. Already the Crown steers might have been swallowed by the *malpais*. If the rustlers had any fear of being jumped there, they might decide to rush the herd on out of the country immediately.

When they had reached Torp's former vantage point and pulled down in the rock field, he said: "You boys wait here. The evidence is all in there, and you shoot the hell out of anybody that tries to get out. I've been in there and can locate the back way easier than you. I'm going on."

"Son," Cal said somberly, "that's the same as riding into a bear cave."

"No way around it. We got to keep that place plugged up till Jack can get back with the sheriff."

He turned to his left, and a little later stretched through the narrow slot he had first used to enter the *malpais*. He had barely passed through the cirque when he heard the sounds of cattle. There he stopped his horse, swung down, and tied the reins to a mesquite bush. He prowled on afoot, his heart beating fast.

As he crept in on the edge of the big, hidden coulée, he got his first estimate of the extent of the gather. It looked much larger than the bunch he had seen driven in. *They're all here,* he thought. That warned him of the shortness of time left to him to locate the back exit and make sure the cattle were not hazed out.

He made his way around the left edge of the steers, digging his boots into the soft talus slope and using the cover of the fallen rocks. He could see nobody but had a feeling that they were all here somewhere. This was too big and dangerous an undertaking for Devers and Campion to entrust it to lesser hands. His feeling grew that, now that the herd was concentrated, it would be moved on without delay.

It seemed a long way around to the north end of the coulée. Yet eventually he began to discern ahead of him a place where the encircling rim seemed to give way. He had to reach it, then hold it as long as his ammunition lasted.

He would have said that it took him an hour to get there, yet he knew that no more than a fourth of that time was required. Once swallowed by the narrow cañon that ran on to the north, he was certain that he was in the right place for his purpose. It was not hard to climb the talus higher and take a station in the rocks. The difficult part was waiting there afterward for the events that were yet to come.

When his ears caught the first warning of approach, the sound came from deeper in the *malpais*. Shoving to a half stand so he could see better, he observed two horsemen coming toward him. His breath caught as he discerned the beard on the face of one of them. There they were: Devers and Arch Campion. They must be scouting the way ahead, getting ready to move again.

For an instant Torp was caught in a half panic of indecision. The sheriff's arrival was hours away yet, at best. This was his chance to cut the head off the rattlesnake. He might stand a better chance of that than holding this cañon against a mass assault. His decision came quickly, and he shoved to a full stand.

"All right, boys . . . lift 'em high!" he rapped.

He had not hoped that they would submit, and they didn't. Arch Campion simply dug his spurs into his horse and sent it sloping forward. Devers whirled his mount, his gun

206

flashing into his hand. Trying to hit and stop Campion's horse, Torp had to ignore Devers for seconds. He shot twice at the fleeing animal, saw it stumble, then resume stride.

He swung back on Devers a split second after the man fired. Torp's hat sailed from his head as he pulled the trigger and saw his own gun gush flame. Devers shot again, but the bullet went low into the talus below Torp's feet. Devers was hit, made a wild grab for his saddle horn, then toppled over and fell to the ground in an inert heap.

Rushing down the slope, Torp took time only to see that the man was really out of the fight. Devers's horse had bolted away, then swung to stare back. "Easy, boy!" Torp coaxed as he slipped toward it. He hadn't much hope of getting hold of a bridle strap, but he made it. Then he swung into leather and started after Campion.

The shooting would have warned the other Rake men here, and might even have carried to Cal and Curly. In any case, the showdown was at hand, and he had to meet it with all he could muster. He yearned to get his hands on Campion before the man managed to slip away somehow.

He hadn't ridden a hundred yards when a gun flash streaked the night ahead of him. In the farther distance he heard shoots rock back and forth. The cattle were already milling in nervousness. Then he saw the downed horse ahead of him, and his excitement climbed high. The animal had quit Campion, who was up in the rocks above. Arch had fired that shot at him, and, even as he realized all this, Torp was pitching from the saddle. The gun ahead blazed again.

Torp heard the bullet's close warning, but by then he was in the rocks and pressed on instantly, relentlessly, his jaw clenched tightly. Campion stopped shooting, his target lost. Torp was heedless in his desire to prevent the man's withdrawing again. Bent low, he ran from rock to rock, always forward, trying to move higher onto the talus than Arch's position.

When he saw his man, Arch was staring hard at the leve just below Torp. Softly Torp called: "Up here, man! This i something I've been waiting for!"

Campion swung, firing at the same time. The bullet tor through the side of Torp's shirt. Torp shot deliberately putting into it all he remembered of this man. Campion' gun hand flung high, the weapon sailing off. He fell back ward.

Torp was standing over him in the space of a breath. He did not realize Campion was alive until the man coughed Hunkering then, Torp rasped: "Where's April Parsons? An swer me, or I'll put another in your belly and make you di hard."

Campion coughed again. "On . . . Crown. She's all . . right. . . ." A paroxysm seemed to seize him then, but it ende abruptly, and he became wholly still.

A sudden, wicked burst of shooting ahead told Torp tha the remaining riders had decided that the trouble was all o this end of the coulée and were trying to break out. They ha run into trouble from Cal and Curly. Again Torp rose to leather and sent his horse streaking in that direction.

But before he had reached the entrance to the coulée, th gunfire had stopped. He rode on cautiously, calling: "Cal . . Curly!"

"That you, Torp?" Cal answered, a moment later.

Cal was not far ahead, and, as he rode on, Torp saw the re sults of that attempt at escape. A man lay on the floor of the narrow cañon, and just ahead was another. The horses appar ently had bolted on through.

Cal and Curly came sliding down the talus as Torp reached the portal.

"One got through," Cal said. "What the hell did you tackle in there?"

"Devers and Campion. They're both dead."

Cal let out a long, tired sigh. "Then it's ended. Bush couldn't ask for any more evidence than's in here. Not that it matters much, except for the record. There's nobody left to hang."

"You boys can handle this. April's being held on Crown. I got that out of Arch before he breathed his last. I'm going there."

"I don't reckon you'll have any trouble," Cal said, "once you tell 'em what happened here."

It was an hour past dawn when Torp rode in to Crown headquarters. His arrival caused as much excitement as it had the last time, but far less hostility. Beaten, baffled men waited there. When he located Brownless, who had been their spokesman previously, Torp rode over to him.

Staring down, he said: "The sheriff'll be out here in another two, three hours. He'll find Campion and Devers dead in the *malpais,* along with a big cut of Slash P and Crown steers. I don't blame you boys for getting your hackles up. You probably don't even know why you're holding April Parsons, and I want her, right now."

Brownless swallowed nervously.

Half a dozen other men shuffled their feet.

"We commenced to figure we'd all been fooled," Brownless said sheepishly, "when Campion led us into that fight, then sneaked away. We was supposed to hold onto April and fetch the rest of you here. But we never aimed to hurt her any. She's locked in a room in the big house. Joe, you go let her out."

A man hurried off.

His voice growing heavy with weariness, Torp said: "You boys ready to help Rita run this spread?"

"You ain't going to?"

"I never intended to."

"Well . . . if she can overlook this, we'd sure like to make amends."

Nodding, Torp rode over to the steps of the big house porch, swung down, and went up the porch steps. April was standing in the doorway.

"It's over . . . ," he began.

"I know. The man told me."

Then she came forward with a rush into his arms. There in the doorway of the house he might have called his own, he caught her hungrily. Then they started down the steps together to go back where they belonged.